THE RAINBOWS END

L A MICHAELS

LML BOOKS

Copyright © 2022 by L A Michaels

First edition published by LML Books May 2022

All Rights Reserved

Cover Design by: PolyArts36

Front cover image by: luviiilove

Back cover image by vwebs123

Edited and proofed by Sandra Watts

OTHER BOOKS BY L A MICHAELS

BETWEEN HEAVEN AND HELL

THE INNOCENT YEARS

THE YOUNGISH MARRIEDS

I LOVE YOU, I HATE YOU, I MISS YOU

TECHNICALLY MAGIC

NOVELAS:

OUR PRIVATE WORLD APART

For my favorite Welsh Boy. Love Always.

From the flames of a fire to the blue skies above, we are all just somewhere Between Heaven and Hell...

HARRY – JUNE 2019

"I think I'm going to have to quit my job. I just don't know what I'm going to do for the rest of the summer," Peter explained to the group.

Owen nodded, "I think it might be for the best. It seems as if they just don't know how to treat you."

Peter rubbed his forehead. "It's just getting to the point where I don't know what else I'm supposed to do. I keep getting shoved on the register over everyone else there. I've seen people go onto the floor over me countless times. I can't handle being called by the wrong pronouns, and then I just get so used to being called by the right pronouns I get all freaked out. Will they start to question... do they think I'm between genders? I can't help the way I speak. I'm not going to lose my hair just to sound deeper at this point," Peter told everyone.

The clock was ticking away, and this was starting to tie a giant knot in Harry Knight's stomach and throat. The curly-haired Knight boy hated public speaking. This included speaking in front of the group. It didn't matter what he had to say. He always came on stumbling out with his words. *Maybe Peter will ramble a bit longer? Oh, that's not nice to say, Harry thought. Well, it doesn't matter! I don't want to talk. I guess I could talk about my vacation, but I don't want to come off as bragging. What if it sounds stupid? What if I come off as being overly excited, and it isn't that exciting?*

The boy continued to look at the clock. *Damn it! he* thought to himself. They would have just enough time. Harry took a deep breath and started to practice in his mind exactly what he would say...

"Thank you for sharing, Peter. I hope that you can find a new and better job," Owen, the leader of the group, said. Owen was in his mid-twenties and a newly licensed therapist. He had replaced Gwen, the group's old leader when she moved to Dallas in the Spring.

Harry was not sure if he liked Owen. Owen would give him these looks, and sometimes his tone of voice would come off in a way that was not very warm, at least not to Harry. It seemed like the others in the group liked him.

"Well, we have just enough time to talk with Harry." Owen turned to the curly haired Knight boy and blinked. The blond man sighed, "Ok, Harry... how about you tell us what you have been up to."

"I've just been, you know... doing the same stuff as usual. I mean just trying to study up for my senior year. You know the same stuff as usual. Preston and I are taking a vacation soon. You know the same stuff as usual. Yeah." Harry realized that he had just said the same thing at least three times. *Damn it!* He wanted to remove himself from the stupid group meeting as soon as he possibly could.

Owen nodded, "Well, thank you for sharing, Harry." He looked down at a clipboard. "I notice that you have been attending the Gay-Straight Alliance for over a year now, it seems. That's an accomplishment."

Why would he say it like that? I mean, it is an accomplishment. It's pretty cool. It's sort of cool. I mean, I think it. It is. Right? Why is Owen bringing this up?

The Knight teen started to dig his fingernails into his arm. He often wondered if anyone ever noticed him doing this. To some degree, he wanted people to notice. He didn't do it because he wanted to harm himself. He did it because he wanted someone to notice. No one ever did. If they did, they just didn't care.

"I guess it is an accomplishment." Harry admitted.

"Well, we are going to wind things down for the day. Please take this time to get to know some of the newer members. It takes courage to come to the meetings, even if you are just an ally. Harry, would you mind sticking around for a second so I could speak with you?" Owen sat up, and this signaled everyone else to break from the circle.

Harry really didn't want to meet with Owen, especially with people around. He didn't understand why Owen would single him out to talk with him like this in front of everyone else. It was kind of a jerk move. At least Harry thought so.

"You wanted to talk," Harry stated, not asked in his usual monotone voice.

The councilor smiled at him. "I just wanted to congratulate you again on coming to the meetings for over a year. I also wanted to point out that your agreement to the organization ended six months ago."

What the hell was that supposed to mean? Harry asked himself. Well, he did know... It was during the court proceedings that Harry had agreed to go to some form of LGBTQ counseling. It was at the judge's request because she felt he needed more confidence in order to keep him away from the occurrence that landed him in court in the first place.

"Well... I mean if you don't want me to come around

anymore… I don't know what you mean," Harry admitted.

Owen gave him a smile that came off as being fake. "Well, it's just you don't come off as wanting to be here. Gwen had mentioned you could come off as stand-offish as well. I just don't want you to be somewhere that you don't feel comfortable."

It might have come off as a kind gesture but what Harry got from this conversation was that Owen didn't like him or his ideas. Oh well, big deal. Harry really wasn't that fond of Owen himself. This just confirmed it for Harry.

"Well, no… I enjoy coming to the meetings. I'll be back after my trip this coming weekend."

"I'm glad to hear that, Harry," Owen said, and he put his hand on his shoulder. Harry automatically stepped back. He wasn't fond of someone touching him who was not his family or Preston, especially not in public places.

He nodded and started to walk away. Harry quickly grabbed his backpack from the floor. It just had a couple of books in it to read before the meeting.

He was always at least a half-hour early. Harry refused to be late for anything. He also preferred to be the first there so that people couldn't judge him walking in after them. It's just how he preferred to do things. *The lighting in this room is terrible… I wonder if I got a text message.* He quickly pulled out his phone. A text from his aunt told him that she and his father missed him and would be back in a few weeks from out of town.

His aunt Vivica Weston had married his father Cliff Knight back in January. The two had been childhood sweethearts and rekindled their love after his aunt's marriage ended. His father's marriage to his mother, Vivica's sister Tiffany started to crumble as well. For a long time as a young child, Vivica was the only mother figure that Harry had known. He had always been closer with his aunt than his mother. In fact, it had been a few months since he had spoken with her. She was off somewhere in the UK working for a private hospital. She was a surgeon.

Harry was essentially left home alone, aside from his older sister Hannah. She was either always at work or with her boyfriend, Xander. Harry spent most of his time with Preston, though. It used to be that Harry spent all his time with his cousin Brad and best friend, Langley. Then Brad cheated on Langley, and Langley fled town in resentment. Harry missed Langley. Brad, in shame, fled back to boarding school himself and was spending time in Canada on a summer trip to avoid being in Grosse Pointe. This was Harry's new normal, which had been his old normal before Brad moved back home. The difference was he had Preston now...

"Hi, Harry!" Gena said as they skipped over. Gena was a bisexual girl that didn't like female pronouns but still identified as female. Harry himself didn't understand it but respected their pronouns. They were a pretty cool person. Gena went to West Grosse Pointe High School, so he really only ever saw them at the meetings. Harry himself went to Saint Agnes Catholic school, which wasn't that far from the public school, really. Gena always wanted to hang out, but Harry just got freaked out over the concept of trying to come up with what he would do with them. Would he invite Preston? Would they go to his house?

"Hey!" he said, trying to sound happy. He wasn't sure what he was today.

"Oh my gosh! You have to come to my end-of-the-year party. I think a few Saint Agnes people will be there. It's going to be fun. You should totally bring Preston. I'm sure the two of you will fit right in with my other friends," Gena explained.

Did she just refer to him as a friend? Harry didn't know what to say or respond with. "I mean, if we can make it." He didn't want to go. He didn't want to interact with strangers and maybe some random people from school. He didn't like new settings.

His phone started to buzz. It was Preston. He was in the parking lot. "I gotta get going," he explained. He waved goodbye to her.

***

I don't have to go to the meetings anymore. Great! I don't want to go to the meetings anymore. I wonder if someone complained. I bet someone complained. I wasn't social enough for someone. It was probably Owen himself. He comes off as such a tool. He is hot, though... What am I thinking?

This was always going on in his mind. Harry thought a million things a minute to the point where he really couldn't stop. At one point, meditation was suggested. He just couldn't figure out how to clear his mind.

The Knight teen walked out from the Grosse Pointe Library. It was a bright and sunny day, and Harry was wearing a bulky dark blue sweater with a light blue button-down. He had skinny jeans that were still too big on him and some white canvas shoes.

Harry tried to style his very curly brown hair before leaving that morning, but it always came off looking the same. The boy hated getting his haircut. It really only stayed styled for a few days if he actively avoided touching it from the time he left the salon. Looks mattered to him, but at the same time, they really didn't.

The black KMC sports car was waiting for Harry in the library parking lot. His own car was in the shop for a day or so. He'd be gone by the time it was done. Preston Costa, the most amazing guy on the planet, offered to pick him up. He waved as he approached the car and promptly got in. "Hi," Harry said nervously, out of breath. He looked at himself for a moment in the mirror. He clearly was blotching red. Whether it was from being in his head or wearing way too many layers in late May, he had no idea.

"So, how was your morning?" Harry asked, still out of breath.

Preston looked at him. At first confused, but then he smiled. "My morning was fine. What happened now?" His boyfriend knew him way too well.

"It's not that something happened. I mean... Owen seems like a nice guy. I've mentioned that before. I mean, really, he is a cool guy. He just comes off like sort of a jerk, and it kind of bothers me," Harry admitted to him with no context of what just happened.

The Costa boy put his hand on Harry's shoulder and started to rub it. "Relax, man. It's a bright and sunny day.

Owen is an asshole. We've already been over this. You don't have to backtrack or apologize for people with shitty attitudes. Just keep saying that to yourself."

Preston started to drive. "So, tell me what stupid thing Owen said this time."

That was the thing. Owen did say a lot of stupid things. At least they were stupid in Harry's mind.

"Well, I mean, he reminded me that I had been going to the meetings for over a year now. Which yeah, I kind of lost track of a while back. He said I didn't have to continue coming if I didn't want to. It's the way he said it," Harry explained.

His boyfriend nodded, "I think that was a jerk thing for him to say. However, do you really want to continue going to the meetings? Do they actually help you?" Preston asked.

Did they help? Harry wasn't so sure. When he first started to go, they were forced upon him. He never really liked wearing his sexuality on his sleeve. Sometimes, it would make him uncomfortable to be around some of the more effeminate guys, which there was nothing wrong with. Harry just liked to blend into the crowd and not be noticed. It was how he spent the first seventeen years of his life. It was how he planned to spend the rest of it if at all possible. He knew that wasn't going to be the case.

"Maybe not, but if I stop going, then Owen wins."

Preston laughed, "Oh, Harry... I don't know what to do with you sometimes." It was the way he said this. It didn't offend Harry in the slightest. It would have offended him if it had come from any other person, aside from maybe Langley. Langley had been just as blunt as Preston had been.

Harry really missed Langley. She was just the only person aside from Preston who really tried to get to know him for him. His sister Hannah always had been there as a confidant and tried her hardest. She just failed, but he still admired her for it. Brad, his cousin, and stepbrother, and best friend, was just so typically masculine himself. He didn't like sharing his feelings. He had two settings; Brad, which was just masculinity to the max, and anger, which was why Brad had exiled himself. Instead of trying to work out his feelings with the people around him, he ran. Yet, Langley did the same. If anything, she was also the definition of masculinity, yet covered it with overly sexualized femininity. Preston was sort of like that himself but was more reserved.

The two boys drove past the Ford mansion. Harry had

been there twice, once on a field trip and once for a boring event his father was invited to. He remembered his mother making sure the entire family looked like a stock photo.

The Knight family and the Fords were in a rivalry that surpassed the feud between the Knight and Fitzpatrick families. The Ford family took claim in Michigan and US history with the Model T. Yet, the Knight family proclaimed behind closed doors that it was their design. The Ford family started a rumor that the Knight family had actually stolen their first models from the Fords. All urban legends. Even so, the Knight family made it their mission to always be above the Fords in sales. It didn't matter if they were second to last on paper in terms of the Big Four. They would make sure they surpassed Ford.

They pulled up to North Pointe. This was the name of the Knight family home. It was just as old and grand, but it wasn't as private as the Ford mansion. The Knights actually lived at North Pointe as well. They lived on a street alongside many other prominent figures and also Mrs. Templeton, but she didn't count.

"My mom wants you to come to dinner tonight," Preston explained to Harry.

"Oh, that sounds fun. Where are we going?" Harry asked.

Preston laughed, "Um, actually, we are just staying in. My dad is cooking, don't worry. My mom isn't really allowed in the kitchen. My sister is spending another week at her boarding school, so we won't have to deal with her. Uncle Jack might stop by, though."

"Wow, um... Yeah. I'm totally down," Harry explained as he looked straight forward at his driveway. This was the first time that he had ever been invited over to Preston's house. They always went out to eat when he was invited to family occasions. Otherwise, Harry and Preston spent all their time at Harry's house, as Preston was always welcomed into his house, especially since Brad left. His aunt Vivica had made it a point to be welcoming towards Preston even though she wasn't at first.

"Do you want me to bring anything?" Harry asked.

"Just your smile," Preston said.

Was this sarcasm? Harry looked at him. "Is it going to be safe?" Harry was just going to be blunt about it.

The smile left his boyfriend's face, "Yeah, I don't foresee anyone bringing us any trouble tonight. My parents wouldn't have invited you if they didn't think you would be safe."

It was hard for Harry to ask that question but also an important one for him to ask. Anthony Costa, on paper, owned a national delivery service. His wife, Jackie Carson-Costa, owned an art gallery. It was well known that the Costa family had mob connections and that Anthony himself was the supposed "God-father of Grosse Pointe". That title might have actually reached out further than that.

Harry knew all the so-called rumors. Preston was nothing like that, though. He wasn't so sure at first, but Preston was simply amazing. The curly-haired boy couldn't help but stick around. It was also a subject the two boys had chosen not to discuss. The few times it did come up, it was always very coded, in the sense that they would discuss his father having a bad day at work or something.

As much as the rest of the town hated the Costa family, Harry didn't see them in the same light. He could obviously tell that Preston's mother was definitely how his aunt Vivica had described her, a neurotic woman who always got what she wanted. He could also tell that Anthony was no-nonsense except when it came to his wife and children. Preston's sister Annabelle was rather uptight, but she was also thirteen years old. Harry had grown up with Hope as a sister, so he was used to uptight people.

"What do you think I should wear?" Harry asked.

Damn it, Langley! Where the hell are you? I mean, I know you are in New York, but I need you here! I wonder if Langley thinks about me ever. I doubt she does. She probably doesn't even remember me. Maybe she changed her phone number, and that is why she isn't responding. She hasn't blocked me on her socials or anything but still. Oh lord...

He started to shake a little bit, and Preston put his hand on his shoulder again.

"I'm sorry. I just..." Harry started to panic.

"Got into your head again. Harry Heathcliff Knight, we have been over this. You are not allowed in your own head from the hours of 12 AM to 11:59 PM." Preston gave him a look of concern. "Just wear what you have on now. If I notice a thing different, then I will force you only then to go change. Now I have to get to tutoring, so I will see you later tonight."

He kissed the curly-haired Knight boy on the lips. It lasted like thirty seconds, but to Harry, it felt like an eternity, and he never wanted it to end. Preston had the softest lips in the world.

Reluctantly the Knight teen got out of the car and waved goodbye. Harry now had the daunting task of figuring out how he would spend the rest of his day until dinner time.

SUSAN – JUNE 1968

Could life be perfect? That was often on the strawberry blonde's mind. Susan Fitzpatrick arched her shoulders back as she looked up at the clouds. It was a rare day when she didn't have to work at the family bar or help out at the family business.

Susan's father was the founder of Fitzpatrick Steel, a company that provided steel to the big four in the auto industry. Knight Motor Company was the first to put them on the map. However, today was not about business. Today was about spending time with her two best friends in the world, Delia Knight, the wife of Benton Knight, who happened to be the current CEO of the Knight Motor Company, and Sister Mary Newman. Mary had been her younger brother's teacher several years back. The three met through Susan's brother, Brandon, and Delia's son, Rodrick, fighting due to words exchanged by Rodrick towards Brandon's now girlfriend Nadia Bloom.

"You have to at least have a sip of this," Delia explained to Mary.

Susan couldn't help but giggle and knew exactly what was on Mary's mind.

"Oh, Delia, I just don't have a taste for alcohol, and I wish you wouldn't either," the nun told their mutual friend.

Delia had a drinking problem. It had gotten better during the years the two women had befriended her. However, it still was not cured. It didn't help that Delia's husband was a flat-out drunk, and the entire town of Grosse Pointe greatly knew it. Small towns spoke, especially, about the most prominent figures in town.

"I suppose it will just be another sip for me," Delia stated, rather excited with that notion. The tan Latina smiled as she took another sip.

Their friendship was definitely odd; a nun, a socialite, and a woman who was just now experiencing life in her mid-twenties. This was definitely always on her mind. It was just surreal.

A familiar young man walked over as they continued to gossip at a tented table at the Grosse Pointe Yacht Club's pool.

"Mother, I'm not coming home tonight," Rodrick explained.

Susan already knew how this one was going to end.

Delia put down her drink. "You will be home by midnight. That's the latest you are allowed out during the summer," the mother told her son.

Susan was not fond of Rodrick. She didn't think anyone was if she were really being honest. It wasn't her place to say anything, though. Susan looked directly at Mary, who kept a straight face during this situation. Mary had the most beautiful eyes. She had beautiful blonde hair as well. It was always covered by a habit, except on rare occasions. There were times that Susan had to ask herself if Mary ever saw her from a vanity standpoint. If she did, then was she pretty in her eyes? The only person that Mary had ever been in love with was God, though.

"I said I'm not going to come home!" the boy screamed and stormed off.

"Well, we should probably get going if we are going to catch that movie," Mary explained, trying to move on from that incident.

Delia rubbed her forehead. "I just don't know what to do with that boy. I don't want him running off like his brother did," the Knight woman told her two friends.

Susan understood, but then at the same time, had no idea what it must be like. She wasn't a mother, and she, unfortunately, probably would never be.

"Is Clifton doing alright in Amsterdam?" Susan now asked.

Now Mary chose to respond with her eyes.

"I mean... I suppose. I only really hear from him through letters. I blame that on Dallas Bolton."

Dallas was her older son, Clifton's wife. Dallas happened to be a black girl from right outside the Grosse Pointe city limits who went to Saint Agnes with Clifton while they were still in school. The Knights were very much against the mixed-race relationship. Delia herself was more concerned with how much Clifton had been into the girl at a young age. It wasn't a race thing for her. Delia happened to Hispanic, which the Knight family did not care for. Her own husband would not even let her embrace her heritage.

"Oh, let's just get going." Delia finished off her drink.

Susan then shot up. "I'll drive," she explained.

Delia shrugged and gave her the keys. "I'm going to use the washroom really quickly," Delia told the two women.

She walked off somewhat tipsy without waiting for a response.

"Why did you bring up Clifton?" Mary asked, a little bit annoyed.

Susan took a short deep breath. "It wasn't intentional," she explained.

Mary put her hand on her shoulder. The Fitzpatrick woman felt a sense of butterflies pounding on her stomach.

"I know you always mean well, but Susan, you have to remember, Delia is loose cannon. The last thing we need is for her to go on another bender. We can't rescue her from the asylum a second time. That place was terrible towards her, and you and I know very well that Benton would love for her to go back so that he can more easily sleep around."

The Knight family were both the wealthiest in town and also the messiest. Their exploits were not those of a functioning family unit.

HARRY – JUNE 2019

North Pointe was the ancestral home of the Knight family. A modest three-story home, not counting the basement. It, of course, had a pool and a guest home and was on Lake Saint Clair itself. The Knight family, being of Knight Motor Company, also had a rather intimidating home garage. This was all sort of lost on Harry, who spent most of his time in his room or in the drawing-room.

The teen entered the home and was lost on the white marble floors and almost gray painted walls. The paint was his mother's doing. It used to be yellow. Admittedly that wasn't much better.

The foyer looked upon the grand staircase which led to the second floor. The open concept dining room was off to the left and the drawing-room to the right. The doors were closed. They had a living room upstairs and a library that was behind the staircase. No one really used the library. It was more or less a space lost in time from the '40s and '50s. It even had a lot of furniture that really hadn't been updated since probably the early '70s. The drawing-room really was the living room, but it had always been labeled as such. This home was stuck in the '50s.

He looked at the family portrait of his great-great-grandparents Heathcliff and Jennifer, his great-grandparents Benton and Delia, and his grandfather and granduncle Rodrick and Clifton. He noticed it was hand-painted, and aside from Jennifer, they all looked terribly miserable.

Misery was a recurring theme in the Knight household. It was almost as if they were all born cursed miserable. It was their job to break the curse individually. It took his great-grandmother, who was married into the family, becoming a widow. It took his own father into his current age with three almost entirely grown children.

What was Harry's misery? He was diagnosed with anxiety very early on in life. That was only the tip of the iceberg though, he was clearly OCD and not a case of *oh, I have OCD, haha*. Oh no, Harry would get freaked out over the most mundane things in the world. Langley had been the first person outside of the family to know about this. She had always been supportive of him, trying to keep him calm while pushing his limits.

Preston went on to be the second. He, much like Langley, tried to test his boundaries and see how far Harry could handle a situation. It would often shock him at just how far it apparently was. The OCD was something that he just couldn't shake, though.

Footsteps were coming from inside the drawing-room, and the door opened. "Oh, hi Harry!" It was the family maid Holly, or, well.... his aunt Vivica's maid... well, best friend that happened to have the title of maid, who he never really saw working a full day in the time that he had known her. "So, have you heard from your aunt? I haven't since yesterday." Holly O'Dell was a dark-skinned beauty with a bachelor's in psychology. She had been working on her masters when she ended up as Vivica's maid. Why she never returned to getting her degree was a mystery to all of them.

"I got a brief text from her this morning. Just checking in." Harry liked Holly, but he didn't understand her a lot of the time. She was married with two kids of her own but spent most of her time at the Knight house. She was originally hired when his aunt was remarried to her first husband, Nial Fitzpatrick, Brad's father. Holly stayed with Vivica throughout that marriage and then the divorce when they moved into Vivica's mansion across the street. Then into North Pointe. Again, he liked Holly, but the friendship was definitely an odd one. "Do you know if the chef went grocery shopping?"

"No idea. He better have, though. I swear the help

around here is so lazy. I need to go clean the toilet or something," Holly explained as she walked upstairs, taking out her phone. Harry had to admire that Holly had no issue with just walking upstairs without any cleaning objects, dressed in clothes that definitely were not made for cleaning. She more than likely was about to go use his father and aunt's Jacuzzi tub or steam shower.

The Knight teen just shook his head and continued to walk towards the kitchen. The kitchen was left off the foyer down a long hallway. At the end of the hallway was the garage. Off to the right was the kitchen itself. You could access the library to the right from inside the kitchen, and there was a back staircase.

He was shocked to see his sister sitting at the kitchen table. "Hey!" Harry said. It was unusual for him to see Hannah at home during the day ever since she took on the VP's position at KMC.

Hannah turned around and smiled at Harry, "Hi stranger!"

Harry quickly walked over to the table and sat down across from his sister. "I'm the stranger? You're literally never home!"

On top of her job, she was dating Xander Kingsley.

Xander was Langley's older brother and was a police officer with the Grosse Pointe Police Department.

Harry admittedly tried to get close with Xander after Langley ran for the hills. Yet there just wasn't much in common between the two men. It also didn't help that before Xander dated Hannah, he had briefly dated Hope. Hannah might not have had an issue with this, but he did.

It was just history repeating itself with his aunt and mother and his father. He didn't blame his father in that situation, though. Harry blamed his mother. Hannah did, too, for that matter. Yet, she continued to keep the tradition of backstabbing alive with her own sister. While Hope had dated Xander first, Xander and Hannah had hit it off first. Hope only seemed to be interested because Hannah was. He supposed the love triangle really wasn't his business. It really didn't matter at all because Hope was living in Europe alongside their mother.

"So, Preston invited me to dinner tonight...at his house."

"That's great!" Hannah said. She seemed to expect there was more to this story.

"I've never been to Preston's house before," Harry stated.

His sister nodded. "Really? Well, that's odd," Hannah said. It seemed like she had more to say but held back.

"I don't know... maybe there was a reason why I wasn't allowed there before? You know, like because of his parents being in the mob?" Harry said aloud.

He knew that Hannah was holding back because he didn't ignite that part of the conversation.

The Knight daughter took a sigh of relief. "Ok... well, I don't want you to take this the wrong way, but what if the reason before was because they were keeping something in that house that people shouldn't see."

It was possible. However, in this town, that wasn't out of the ordinary. Mrs. Templeton, who lived down the street, had pet squirrels and a Filipino housekeeper obsessed with making pie, who only left the house at nighttime. Even then, she was seldom seen.

"Do you think I'm going to be alright with Preston alone for a week?" Harry randomly blurted out. He needed the perspective of someone on this. He had been dating Preston for almost nine months.

Hannah and the rest of his family were the only people who had ever been on vacations with him. He had no idea what it must have been like to go on vacation with someone that was always freaking out about one thing or another.

His sister looked down and then back up and then did the same again. "It's not my place to tell you what to do in this situation, Harry. I think you have done a lot of work on your anxiety. So, as long as you remember to do what the doctors have told you and take your medications when you are supposed to, you should be fine."

Why was it whenever this subject was brought up, whether to his family or to a therapist, he always got the same response regardless of what the actual question was.

He had made progress... *Am I actually making progress? Will I ever be able to live a normal life? I just want to be loved. It's too early for Preston to admit his feelings for me. I can't tell him that I love him. It just would put pressure on him.*

All of a sudden, a second voice popped into his head. *Get out of your head Harry!* Harry looked around the room. Langley? He thought to himself. Where on earth was her voice coming from.

He rubbed his forehead, "I just don't want to put him down the entire week."

"You aren't going to do that. He knows you at this point. Has it affected your relationship with him?" Hannah asked her brother.

Had it? He wasn't really sure. Yes, he had gone on manic episodes in front of Preston. Preston just usually rolled with it. Harry just didn't like the idea of Preston having to stop enjoying himself all week every time something would freak him out, or he got too in his head. *Harry, so help me... just be you... Preston likes you!* Langley screamed in his head.

Harry was starting to get a bad headache. "I need to lay down for a little bit," he told his sister.

"Alright. Well, tell me if you need anything. When you get back, we are totally having a Hannah and Harry day! We could always go and visit Brad as well," Hannah offered.

Hannah was a good sister. She only ever wanted what was best for him. There were just times that no one in his family really knew how to handle it when it came to him. It was what it was.

This was so weird. He was hearing Langley's voice in his mind. Sure, he remembered how Langley spoke. It had only been about four or five months since she had left. She had called a few times, but their scattered communication mainly had been through one-off texts. He walked up the back staircase of North Pointe. He felt dizzy. As he made it into his room, he walked into his bathroom and looked in the mirror. It was like he didn't recognize himself. Yet, he was staring right at himself, and it was indeed him.

For a brief moment, he felt as though the blonde-haired, blue-eyed teenage girl known as Langley Lorelei Kingsley was behind him, but it only lasted a brief second. It was just his mind playing tricks with him.

"Langley is in Manhattan or something. She doesn't live here anymore, and she probably won't return. You need to move on, Harry," he said this out loud.

He needed to stop thinking about Langley. It was easier said than done. She had been his best friend, and his first best friend who was not related to him, was Brad. Why did Brad have to cheat on Langley? Why did Harry feel like it was partially his fault for the entire ordeal? He knew that was silly. It had nothing at all to do with him. Brad let another girl seduce him, and Langley was too smart not to figure out what was going on.

Distraction... I need a distraction. The Knight son walked back into his bedroom and sat on the bed. He couldn't just sit in silence, so he turned the TV on to drown out the now multiple voices in his head. That reality show about the Drag Queens started to play on the TV.

"Pass," he quickly turned the channel to some kids' network. It was mindless noise that wasn't likely to upset him. It wasn't working. He grabbed his tablet from his nightstand and opened it. He needed to do something. Anything... Harry sighed. He typed in *hot teen guys shirtless* in the search bar. Is this really where he was going to go with this? Yes, he needed to relieve himself before he went to dinner with Preston. Harry had a few hours to go down the rabbit hole.

SUSAN – JUNE 1968

"**S**usan, where have you been? I have to get home to start dinner for your father's business meeting," her mother Ida stated in a panic.

Susan took off coat and put it on a hook.

She was in the kitchen of the bar that her family had inherited. Susan was essentially running it at this point, alongside her mother with a little help from her brother. Her father, Seamus, had stopped working there once the family steel company started making money.

A small part of Susan just wanted to take over the bar outright. However, her parents would more than likely veto this in a second.

The strawberry blonde daughter sighed. "I slept in a little. It was a late night with the girls," Susan explained.

Ida sighed. She put on a slight smile. "I like that you finally have some people in your life, but you need to remember family obligations," Ida explained as she put on her coat. "I'll leave leftovers in the kitchen if you are hungry when you get off of your shift."

Ida kissed her daughter and dashed out the back door.

A few months ago, they finally saved up enough money to be able to justify a second car, used, of course. Her father was very frugal.

"It's time for another wonderful shift," Susan said under her breath.

The door that separated the kitchen from the bar opened. It was Nadia Bloom, Brandon's girlfriend.

Susan liked Nadia, but she was definitely a bit of a hellfire. Their mother, Ida, did not like how free-thinking she was about women and their place.

The Fitzpatrick daughter enjoyed her modern viewpoints. It was a nice change from Mary and Delia, who viewed things from an old-world standpoint, which made sense. Mary was a nun, and the church made it very clear what a woman's role in life was. On the other hand, Delia needed to be yanked away from those views. She was not benefiting from thinking a certain way anymore.

"Susan, thank goodness you are here. I need your

advice," Nadia explained.

Susan smiled that Nadia would seek her out for advice.

"What kind of advice?" she asked. Nadia took a deep breath. "Should I break up with your brother if he keeps talking about marriage? We aren't even out of high school yet, and he wants to get engaged," Nadia said as she sat down at a table in the kitchen.

There wasn't really an answer that Susan could possibly give that wouldn't be biased.

Brandon had definitely inherited a lot of ideas from their father. Luckily the positive views. He wanted to be married right away, though, which made sense. Nadia was a beautiful girl. She had the most beautiful brown eyes, and her hair was so shiny. Susan could understand why her brother would be attracted.

"I think you just need to tell him to be a bit slower in his approach to the next step," she explained to Nadia.

"I want more drinks!" screamed a familiar voice in the next room.

"Oh great, Mrs. Templeton is still here," she sighed.

"She's been here at least since my shift started," Nadia said.

She walked back out into the bar area. The older Fitzpatrick child took a deep breath. This was going to be a long night. She wished she could have spent the day with Mary and Delia again. Delia had to be home herself, though, to tend to her idiot husband.

Since her father-in-law passed away, North Pointe, the ancestorial home of the Knight family, had sort of gone into chaos. As toxic of a person as Heathcliff was, he held the family together. Things did not improve at all for them when Clifton had moved away. If anything, it had gotten worse.

Now she had to worry about Nadia potentially breaking up with Brandon. She always had a loving relationship with her younger brother, but they weren't close by any means. They had an age difference. Susan had to be more of a parental figure in many ways. It wasn't that Seamus and Ida had been neglectful. At least she didn't see them that way.

It was the fact that Seamus had spent the majority of his adult life trying to be as wealthy as the Knight family. They were finally considered middle class and potentially on their way to upper-middle class. Susan honestly didn't care. Brandon clearly didn't either. Money didn't matter to either Fitzpatrick child.

PRESTON – JUNE 2019

Was he going to change his room completely for Harry, or would he keep it looking exactly the same? This was the question that Preston had been asking himself since he finally decided it was time now that Harry is invited inside his house.

It was time. They were together for almost nine months, and in that time, they dodged several parts of his life that Preston probably should have mentioned months earlier.

The Mobster's son sighed. Harry was the overly anxious one, yet in this situation, he was about to give himself an anxiety attack.

There was a knock at his door.

"Come in," Preston said.

"Are you going to pick Harry up soon?" Jackie asked her child.

The boy nodded. "Yeah, I'm just not sure if he is ready

for all of this."

Jackie Carson-Costa put her hand on her hip and flipped her blonde hair. "If that Weston boy has an issue with you, being you, then he isn't worth it."

Preston was aware that in his mother's perfect world, he wouldn't be dating a Weston, as she put it. He explained to her on many occasions that even though, yes, Harry was a Weston by blood, he was also a Knight. That didn't really make her feel any better about it.

It was bizarrely the same situation for Harry and his father and aunt. His sister Hannah seemed to be the only one who tried to act the most normal around them. It wasn't that his father Cliff didn't try, he was just clearly not used to Harry being around anyone, let alone that person being a guy.

Then there was Aunt Vivica. That woman was indeed as crazy as his mother had made her out to be. She was nice to some degree, like when he was first trying to get Harry to like him... or well feel comfortable around him and decided to ask him to the school dance. His aunt had put out a copy of the movie *Xanadu,* and Preston recognized it.

He loved bad movies, and it briefly excited him that Harry was a fan of the movie too. It turned out that Harry had never seen the movie when he showed up at Harry's house and did a roller disco number to ask him to the damn dance. Harry did say yes, though.

"I'm sure he will be fine with it," Would he, though? Even though Harry was gay, he just gave these vibes that he wasn't comfortable with his sexuality in the slightest. It was as if the cat was out of the bag, so he had no choice but to be gay. That said, it was only upon coming out that he really developed friendships with people and came out of his shell. His anxiety took him to some dark places that could admittedly scare Preston. He had to admit, though, that dealing with Harry's issues kept him out of his own head. A part of himself that he had yet to really discuss with Harry...

SISTER MARY NEWMAN
– JUNE 1968

Grosse Pointe and Saint Agnes had not been the young nun's first choice when it came to congregations. If anything, she was tricked into going to Saint Agnes at first.

The first few months had been rather miserable. It was upon meeting Susan that things started to look up. Her friendship with Susan had been so out of leftfield for her and unexpected. Susan was not a particularly religious person. She was also very quiet, which drew Mary to her in many ways.

The school part of Saint Agnes was closed during the summer. A few programs did go on in the school but only during the day. However, Mary still had access to her classroom.

The nuns lived all together in a house a block away from the church and school buildings.

Her roommate, Sister Hattie Maden, was the town

gossip if there ever was one. Mary could only listen to so many stories that started with *"Forgive me for gossiping father but..."*

Sadly, Hattie was the only other nun in her age group. The older nuns were even more gossipy and much more judgmental amongst each other. She knew that none of those women liked that she spent time with a wealthy Knight nor, as the nuns and most of the town put it, the gold-digging Fitzpatrick's.

She knew that judgment was a large part of her religion. However, Mary had a very different view than a lot of her peers. She believed that everyone should be loved. Just as she was thinking this, she could hear a door slam in the hallway. The young nun got up to investigate, opening her classroom door and walking into the hallway, when she was startled as she bumped into...

"Benton Knight?" Mary said, confused. "What are you doing here so late?" She had a curious look on her face. "What are you doing here at all?" It was the summertime and nighttime, after all.

The smug man scoffed. "I just had a meeting with someone. Not that it is any of your business," he explained.

The nun knew that he was lying about something.

She wasn't about to question him. Not because of her friendship with his wife, but mostly because she didn't like him regardless.

"Well, you should really be on your way," Mary said as they both stood in the dark hallway.

"I suppose I will see you lounging around my house soon enough with my drunk wife," Benton said snippily.

Mary put a smile on her face. "I'm sure you will see me around your loving wife, Delia, who I am sure is missing you dearly right now." She couldn't help but roll her eyes at this.

The two walked past one another. Mary would keep that to herself. She, however, wanted to know what he was doing here. He had to have been in the room next to her own. She walked over and opened the door. It was still unlocked, which didn't shock her. A man was sitting at the desk.

"I'm sorry. Who are you?" she demanded.

She knew who he was. He was Jeromy Costa, one of the Costa brothers and essentially a low-level goon at that.

"Name is Costa. I was just conducting a little... after-school extra credit session," he said as he stood up.

The man was chiseled and was wearing a brown leather jacket with a white dress shirt and black tie. An average person would be afraid of a Costa. They were, of course, a known mob family.

"I'll have to ask Father Curtis about your little class," Mary told him.

Jeromy laughed, "I don't think we need to get the father involved."

He had a wise guy voice about him. Most of the current generation of Costa's were born and raised in Michigan. Their New Yorker accents never made a lick of sense to anyone in town.

PRESTON – JUNE 2019

What was taking Harry so long? Preston texted Harry to come out ten minutes ago. He hoped that the Knight boy hadn't gotten freaked out about tonight. The concept of dinner wasn't that big of a deal. It was the news that Preston had not yet shared with Harry that was going to be the big picture we see from all of this.

Finally, the front door opened, and Harry emerged. He was wearing a completely new outfit. Preston would just pretend that he hadn't probably had spent the last two hours changing. He didn't need to insight an argument with his boyfriend since it wasn't that big of a deal, if at all.

Harry opened the door and got into the passenger seat. Preston gave him a kiss on the cheek, "What the heck took you so long?"

"Holly wouldn't stop asking questions about my aunt. She is concerned about her or something," the Knight teen explained.

The Mobster's son had to admit he didn't understand the dynamic between Holly the maid and Vivica, his aunt.

"She knows that she could just stay home until Vivica gets back. I mean, it isn't like Holly does any actual cleaning."

"I mean, you have a good point, but I tend to leave that argument alone with the two of them. I like Holly. She has always been really nice," Harry admitted.

To some degree, Preston understood the dynamic. It was like his uncle with the family. He was always around. Though his uncle had actual business ties to the family.

He started to drive. It was about five minutes back to his house, where things would change forever.

"So, then I'm excited to show you, my room."

It was apparent the curly-haired boy was starting to blush. "I mean, I'm excited to see it as well."

"I don't mean it like that," although Preston would love to explore that as well. He knew that tonight definitely wasn't going to be the night that happened. The two of them hadn't gone past getting shirtless with one another. It was almost a mutual unsaid agreement. Preston felt weird being even shirtless to some degree, but Harry seemed to like his body.

Preston knew he was in good shape. It just sometimes felt weird to be shirtless around people.

Getting changed in the locker room had always been a conflict for him. He knew he had a good body. Yet, there had always been a sense of not feeling comfortable flaunting it. Was it even flaunting? Was getting changed in the locker room or going swimming flaunting something? Preston sometimes didn't know. He was often reminded of when he first met Harry. It was at the yacht club pool, which he still remembered rather well in his head...

PRESTON -- AUGUST 2018

His parents forced him off the property for the afternoon. They claimed it was because they thought he was spending far too much time at home. Preston assumed there was more to it than that.

He contemplated playing a round of golf at the course, but he was feeling far too lazy to do that. Instead, he chose to go to the Grosse Pointe Yacht Club.

This was really his first time getting out of the house and being around town. Italy had been a wild ride for the teenage boy. He experienced his first love and heartbreak there. It was something that Preston would never regret. It was where he really started to discover himself as a person.

Preston had to admit that there were definitely some attractive people in Grosse Pointe. He also had to admit that he was rather horny after being locked away by choice in his house for months. He wanted to mess around with someone, but who? It would have been easy to find a girl that wanted to piss off her father, but that was the thing, he wasn't looking for that kind of experience. Those were the kind of girls who went after him before he left.

Preston also had to admit that he wasn't sure he wanted to play the part of the pitcher. He wanted to explore the concept of being the catcher. Preston wanted the feeling of a man on top of him. That was when he saw him; the dark curly-haired boy with the most alluring blue-grey eyes he had ever seen. He was rather skinny and pale, but it turned him on. It couldn't be... It was Harry Knight. They had gone to Saint Agnes together before Preston had transferred schools.

Harry was quiet if he remembered correctly. Not really someone who was known to have a good conversation with. He didn't think that he would be rude, though. Preston honestly had tried several times over the years to spark a conversation with the boy. Preston also knew that Harry was out, as he had seen the video. Who hadn't seen the video?

He felt bad for the guy, though. It was sick what that guy did to him, and he didn't know the boy that did it.

A blonde girl was sitting next to the Knight boy. She was pretty herself but looked like a handful. It confused Preston about what she would be doing around Harry. Harry only ever hung around his cousin and whomever his cousin might have hung around.

Preston was not very fond of Brad Fitzpatrick. The two had a bizarre history. Their fathers were lifelong friends. Their mothers hated one another with a passion. His mother also wasn't fond of his father. Vivica Fitzpatrick was notorious in the Grosse Pointe social scene. It was often joked about in hush that his father could get away with so much around town because Vivica kept the gossip mill focused on her. It was also joked about that Vivica preferred it that way.

Preston couldn't imagine that anyone would ever want the spotlight on them as much as Vivica seemed to. Yet, he had also spent more time than he ever wanted to with the woman. It was more than likely true.

The Costa teen felt ambitious. He was going to walk up to the two teens. The blonde girl seemed to be on a speed talking challenge or something because her mouth kept moving. Harry seemed to be looking in his direction, but not really. He approached them.

"Do you need anything?" the blonde girl asked.

She sort of had this *I'm better than you* attitude about her. He was definitely going to steer clear from flirting with her. He turned his attention to Harry.

"Oh, I just wanted to say hi. We go to school, together,

right?" Why did he say that? Obviously, they went to school together. At least they used to go to school together and would again.

"Um, well... sort of," Harry mumbled. He now seemed to be awkwardly avoiding Preston. It sort of turned the Mob boy on but also fascinated him. It was so bizarre. There was something about this boy.

The blonde sighed, "If you go to Saint Agnes, then yes, he goes to school with you. I will be attending there as well in the fall. I'm Protestant, though." She explained.

This was all useless information to him.

"You're Harry Knight, right?" as he kept his focus on the Knight boy.

Harry blinked, "Yes." He seemed annoyed by this question. Preston was unsure if he wanted to continue talking with him if this was going to be the way he spoke. Yet, he didn't want to go away.

"So, what is it like to be the son of a criminal?" What the hell did this girl just ask?

"My father was involved in the New York Mob scene from a financial standpoint. Probably won't be seeing him anytime soon."

Preston crossed his arms. "Who said my family was involved in any crimes? My mother owns an art gallery, and my father is in the shipping business," the teen said rather proudly. It was true, after all.

The blonde rolled her eyes, "So, then, when are we hanging out? I'm casually seeing Brad Fitzpatrick, and Harry is single. Three's a crowd, but four is a party. You should come over to Brad's house tonight for an after-dinner swim. Doesn't that sound fun?"

"I will consider it." With that, Preston turned around. It seemed like the blonde girl was the one he had to get to in order to be around Harry. The only issue was that she was seeing Brad. She didn't seem to be the wet blanket type. He was definitely going to hang out that night. There was no doubt about it. He wanted to get to know the boy with the alluring eyes more than ever now...

PRESTON -- JUNE 2019

So much had changed for the young couple since they had first met. Preston went from lusting after him to falling deeply for him. Despite their family dramas, both mutual and apart.

"What are you thinking about?" Harry asked him. Preston turned. He realized that he had gotten deeply in his head. He parked his car in the driveway. "I was thinking about you, actually."

"Oh boy, what did I do?" Harry asked, a little freaked out. "You can tell that I changed. I just wanted to take a shower after I got home." That seemed like a lie, but again Preston wasn't going to press about his change in clothes. It wasn't a big deal.

He rolled his eyes, "Just breathe, my Knight."

Preston hugged him from the driver's seat. He knew that the best way to calm Harry down was to hug the overly anxious boy.

"Now come on. Let's go inside." They both exited the car. He could tell that Harry was nervous, but he probably wasn't the most nervous for once.

They walked up the front entrance, and Preston opened the door with his key. The house was clean. It wasn't as if he was worried about it that much, though.

His father was into darker walls and floors as well as furniture. But it was his mother who had been put to the task of decorating the house. The foyer was a much more closed concept than most of the mansions in the town. The master staircase was in the living room. The kitchen was down the hall. His father's office was right up front. It was closed, and no one was in there now.

They only had one maid, and she had worked for them for years. His father did the cooking when he was home; otherwise, they ordered out. Preston could smell steak. It smelled great. He knew that Harry was overly nervous as usual, so he took his hand.

"Why don't we go up to my room first?"

"Don't we need to check in with your parents?" Harry asked.

The Crime Boss's son looked at his boyfriend.

"When have we ever checked in with your parents at your house?" Harry shrugged.

It was obvious that Harry expected this trip to his bedroom to be filled with lust and sex. Instead, it was going to be filled with a reveal. The two boys walked up the staircase, and while neither spoke, it was obvious that the flight of stairs was the longest journey either boy had ever taken. His room, of course, had to be at the furthest end of the hallway.

Preston took a deep breath...

"Well, here it is. My room."

HARRY – JUNE 2019

lease, Preston, don't try to get me in bed. I'm not ready to sleep with you. Please don't expect sex... I want you so badly, but I just don't think I'm ready.

He is going to hate me. He is totally going to hate me. Fuck! Fuck, fuck, fuck, fuck!

Harry's eyes widened as the door widened open. He expected a rather ordinary room. It was, but it felt off to some degree. There was a gay pride flag above his bed. That didn't shock Harry. He figured his boyfriend had something like that. It actually looked like the one that Preston had gotten for him to hang in his own room. Harry just wasn't about bright colors.

The curly-haired boy turned, and he saw a shelf with doors on it. It had windows, though, so you could see what was in it. Dolls? Were those dolls? Harry sort of just walked up to them.

"Are these yours?" Harry asked.

His boyfriend took a deep breath.

"Yeah, this is what I was sort of nervous about you seeing. I collect dolls, Harry... I know it's weird."

They seemed to be *Barbie-like* in appearance. He wasn't entirely sure if they were or not. He had never really been around dolls aside from when his sisters were younger. Harry himself had never been that much into them.

"I mean, it's cool, I guess. They aren't in the box. Doesn't that hurt their value?"

"Eh... I don't really collect for selling value," Preston admitted.

Harry had to admit that this was kind of off-putting. He just assumed that there would be a money story behind this. His father had a comic book collection that he insisted was worth something but really wasn't.

"They do have value to them."

His boyfriend opened up the shelf and took one out. It had a very life-like face to it.

"This one's name is Clarissa New. It's the name that she comes with. I don't name them myself. She is one of my favorite sculpts, though. They are luxury dolls. They aren't cheap, and they go up in value as well."

He nodded. This was definitely not something that he had expected Preston to be into. That was fine with him.

"Did you think I was going to have a problem with this or something?"

Why did it seem like Preston was freaked out that he would take issue with something like doll collecting? I mean, it wasn't as if he had an interest in it himself, but he also didn't have an interest in football which Preston happened to play. Langley was insistent that landing a football player was a status symbol, but he didn't care. Harry liked Preston because he was Preston. There really wasn't anything that his boyfriend could tell him that was going to shock him.

"Why don't you tell me more about them?"

"Oh yeah, totally!" Preston stated with glee in his voice.

There was something still off about this. It wasn't the dolls, though, that seemed to be off. It was Preston himself.

Harry picked up one himself.

"Is this a Clarissa?" It was a red-haired doll that almost looked like his aunt in a weird way. "She looks…"

"She isn't a Clarissa. She is a Priscilla Jane. She is based on a 90's supermodel," Preston admitted.

It was as if he knew what he was going to say. This doll was totally inspired by his aunt, which actually was pretty cool. It was a bit bizarre that Preston, of all people, had a doll based on his aunt. He just assumed that a Vivica-inspired doll would be something off-limits in this house.

"Why didn't you tell me about these before?" Harry asked.

Did Preston think that he was going to have an issue with him collecting dolls? It was definitely different but not out of the ordinary.

His boyfriend sat down on his bed, and Harry sat next to him. Preston looked guilty of something, but there was nothing to be guilty about.

"I don't know. You just come off as being kind of conservative sometimes."

Harry's eyes opened wide, "What? I'm not a republican!"

He didn't really follow politics one way or the other if he really thought about it, because it just freaked him out.

He did know that the Republicans usually didn't have very nice things to say or do with gay people, though, so, he just automatically counted them out. He really wasn't sure if the democrats were any better.

His family was traditionally republican, but his father was a democrat. His aunt was also a democrat. Hannah had campaigned rather hard during the last election, from what he remembered. He honestly wasn't sure about his mother. Harry feared thinking to be honest, as she had not been very supportive when he was outed, neither had his other sister Hope. They both currently lived in Europe and had little to no communication with him. Hannah felt this was a good thing. His aunt agreed about that, at least in terms of his mother.

"Do I come off as a republican?" Harry asked this a bit in shock.

Preston shrugged, "I'm not saying you are. I honestly don't know. I mean, is it a deal-breaker for me if you were? I-I just don't know to be honest."

What? Deal-breaker? Harry literally never spoke about politics. "I'm not! Why do you think I'm a republican?"

Did he come off as racist or something? *Is this because we have a black maid? She doesn't do anything! If anything, my aunt pays her to be her best friend. Heck, most of my aunt's friends are black if I really think about it. My great aunt is black. Why am I trying to justify that I'm not a racist? I'm not! Also, none of what I'm thinking is appropriate. Get out of your head Harry!*

"Harry, you really don't come across as liking the fact that you are gay," Preston admitted out loud.

This made the Knight boy turn pale white, and his blood turned cold. He didn't like being gay?

"But I am gay! Preston, I love... I mean, I really like being with you." It was too early to use the word love. At least he thought it was. Was it, though? "You have been one of the most amazing things to ever happen to me."

His boyfriend smiled, "Harry, I love being with you as well. I don't question the fact that you and I care deeply for one another. I just question if you are comfortable with being in the queer community."

That word... it just didn't sound right to Harry. Preston knew that about him.

"I just don't see a reason to flaunt my sexuality. It's just that, "my" sexuality. I can't help but be attracted to guys. It doesn't mean that I need to march around town screaming it. It's not like straight people do that. Well, I guess Mrs. Templeton, but that is about it."

The Costa teen sighed, "Straight people set the standard, Harry. We are technically repressed. People have preferred we stay quiet for years. It's only within the last ten years that queer people have said screw it and live their lives more openly."

"Preston, there have been "out" gay people for much longer than the last ten years," Harry said, a bit confused by this statement.

"Yes, a few have had the courage. It goes far beyond just sexuality, though. You have to think about trans people and people who don't conform to either gender or what we deem the normal sexualities. Everything is still so new for everyone," Preston explained to his boyfriend.

A loud ping came across the room.

"Boys, why don't you head downstairs! Dinner should be done in a few minutes!"

Harry looked around the room. That was Jackie's voice, but she clearly wasn't in the room or at the door.

The Mobsters son started laughing, "We have an intercom system, for safety reasons."

He took Harry's hand. It was obvious this conversation was far from over. Harry understood why Preston was passionate about this. It was the same reason that the Gay/Straight Alliance Group was so passionate about it. They were proud of all of this.

Harry wasn't ashamed of the fact that he was gay. He just felt that if he were straight, the world would be at least slightly easier for him. That's one of the reasons he had been so afraid to come out. In his mind, you could be gay but being gay with anxiety? That was just a bingo card for a chocolate mess.

DELIA – JUNE 1968

"I don't care what you want for dinner. This is what we are having," the mother told her child. "Our cook spent time on this, and you are going to like it."

She didn't even want to eat it if she was honest. Porkchops were Benton's favorite. Everyone else hated them.

"Where is dad?" Rodrick spat out.

If she knew, she would tell him. "Probably at work," the Knight mother explained, which he probably wasn't.

Her marriage had been crumbling for years. Delia thought that things had actually improved when they moved into North Pointe. However, once Benton's father passed on, things got dicey again.

Benton hadn't been defending Delia out of love; it was out of his disdain for Heathcliff. It was not lost on her that they lost the ability to see their own son daily because of similar bigotry. Delia knew that she was in the wrong, but by the time she realized this, it was too late.

"Is dinner done?" her husband asked as he tumbled into the dining room.

She had just had the entire dining room and drawing rooms redone lately. It was a project to keep her out of her head and away from the bottle. She thought that yellow walls looked charming.

"I'm starving," Benton explained as he sat down at the table.

He sat across from Delia. The table sat twelve, six on each side. Rodrick was in a middle seat on the left side, so there was a distance between all three family members.

"I wanted pork chops for dinner. I told the cook before I left," Benton rambled out.

The wife sighed, "That was two days ago, and you threw the plate at him when it wasn't prepared right. So, he is on a paid vacation."

She took a bite of her meal. "So, I made dinner."

She looked up at Benton, hoping that there would be

some approval from him.

He started to laugh. "Well, that explains why it tastes so bad then," her husband told her.

She was used to this at this point.

"I'd have to agree," Rodrick told his own mother. He looked at her in embarrassment.

She wanted to cry, but the phone rang. A maid or the estate manager would pick it up. Delia didn't dare pick it up. If she did, she would have to listen to a speech about how they have a staff for things like that. It had been years since they moved in, and she still wasn't used to this world.

"I ran into your little nun friend today. She was being nosy as usual," Benton explained.

Rodrick groaned. "I hate that you are friends with one of my teachers. It just seems so pedestrian," her son told her.

Delia looked at him, "Your friend group leaves much to be desired."

She then turned to her husband, "Yours as well."

She took a sip of her drink. Iced tea.

"Mrs. Knight, you have a call," their house manager explained.

She sighed. Delia knew the proper response was to take a message. She was over with family time, though.

"I'll take it in the drawing-room," she said.

The wife and mother got up from her seat. She walked out into the foyer and crossed over to the drawing-room where she slammed the door behind her.

"Don't choke up. You don't know who is on the other end. It could be one of those bitchy society women looking for a donation."

She looked at herself in the mirror and put on a fake smile. People in this town knew when you weren't smiling. Even if just on the phone.

"Hello. Delia Knight speaking… Oh, thank goodness it's you, Susan. You want me to come by? Yes. Most definitely yes!"

She hung up the phone without saying goodbye.

Delia got up from the couch and opened the door again. Instead of going back to the dining room, she went straight up the grand staircase. She peaked at the family portrait that was done a few years back. It featured Benton and herself, along with their sons and Heathcliff. She hated that thing so much. It was disturbing to look at. They all looked lifeless and as if they hated one another, which might have been true if she was being honest with herself.

She turned to the right wing and went into her room. She grabbed her purse and a headscarf. She wrapped the scarf around her head and put her purse on her arm. She would have their driver take her to the bar.

As she walked back downstairs, Rodrick walked out of the dining room. "Where the hell are you going?" he asked.

She turned to him very briefly. "Since when do you care?" The mother rolled her eyes at her son and left.

Rodrick turned and looked at his father. They both shrugged in confusion.

HARRY – JUNE 2019

The Costa dining room was decorated like the rest of the home. Harry thought it was calming. A lot like his aunt's old house. Unlike his own house, where it was just so cold.

The Fitzpatrick family home had a similar cold feeling. Yet, at the same time, it felt like the Costa home had more secrets and layers to it than any of the other prominent homes in Grosse Pointe.

"This is really good," Harry said as he looked towards Anthony Costa.

Anthony smiled and looked at his wife, "See, and you were afraid that I was going too extravagant!" he laughed.

His wife laughed back and looked at Harry.

"We just didn't know what would be too much. Preston mentioned that steak was a favorite of yours. When Anthony gets in the kitchen, though, he tends to go to town."

It was obvious that Preston's parents loved one another on another level. Harry was not sure this was a good thing or a bad thing. It was as if the couple thrived off the trauma of their own past. This was something that Harry could tell his own father and aunt were unable to do. It was possible that his aunt Vivica and his cousin's father Nial might have actually thrived in this same way, but because his father Cliff existed in the picture, they were unable to ever really make it work.

"Yeah, I mean, give me a good piece of meat, and I'll devour it," Harry stated as he started to blush the moment, he said this out loud.

"So, we are going to be leaving on Monday then," Preston immediately stated.

His mother smiled, "This is going to be so fun for the two of you."

She looked at Harry. "So, has Preston revealed any of the places that he plans on taking you?"

No, Preston had not, which of course, gave Harry major anxiety because he didn't know how to prep for any of it.

"Not yet. Any chance that you will be giving me any clues," he looked at his boyfriend.

Preston shook his head, "Nope! It's all part of the surprise. I know you will love it, though."

That was the million-dollar question. Would he really love it? Was there anything to really love about this situation overall? Harry hated being surprised, which Preston damn well knew. So, what happens if they show up at something along the way that would freak him out? Would he be able to actually move on? Or would he spend the rest of the trip in a state of shock? It wasn't that he was worried that they were going to do something like go rock climbing.

Then again... *Oh boy... He won't take us rock climbing, would he? He knows I don't like heights. I should have just OD'd myself on Xanax and let him take me to Europe or something. At least then, there wouldn't be that much room for shock. Oh, lord, what if the plane went down, though? Get out of my head! Damn it! Fuck! Get out of my head!*

"I guess I'll find out on Monday then," Harry laughed.

SUSAN – JUNE 1968

I'm just telling you that maybe you don't need to smother her," Susan tried to explain to her brother as she wiped down the bar.

Thus far, it was a relatively slow night. Brandon wasn't even working. He just was bored.

Nadia turned down the suggestion to go on a date and instead spent time with her mother and younger brother DJ. She claimed that it was because her stepfather David Brash was out of town, but Susan knew otherwise.

Brandon twirled around on a bar stool. He had a lot of childlike qualities still, even at seventeen.

"Oh, come on, sis. Nadia knows that I don't smother her," as he brushed back his curly red locks.

Susan sighed, "Just try to give her a little bit of space when she needs it." Susan tried being coy with him, but it wasn't working.

"I need another drink!" screamed Mrs. Templeton.

Susan filled a glass of beer. She had no idea why an old bat like Mrs. Templeton liked beer.

Brandon grabbed it from her hand, "I'll take it over."

Susan would have argued had it been any other customer, but Mrs. Templeton was a special case. The woman had something against her. Susan knew what it was, but she didn't want to confront her about it formally.

She remembered several years back when Mrs. Templeton called her out on it. She was at the Harbor Inn, and Mrs. Templeton accused her of being a lesbian, which back then she hadn't realized that she was, but now, yes. Susan knew she was a lesbian.

Susan was perfectly fine with being a lesbian. However, she had a feeling that her family would have other opinions and her friends.

Delia's family already hated Susan, and Mary was a nun. She suspected that Brandon and even Nadia would not have an issue with it. They had alluded to it several times over. Still, a part of Susan wished she could just be an out and proud lesbian, but not in this town. It was just not something that could be done.

The front door opened, and Delia marched in. A sort of elegance entered the room with her as the door closed. Mrs. Templeton squirmed at the dusk of natural lighting.

"Thank goodness you called!" she practically sang as she sat down at the bar, "I need a drink."

Susan looked at her, and the two women were essentially thinking the same thing.

"I'll have an iced tea," Delia said with a frown on her face.

Susan nodded. "I think an iced tea sounds great right now!" Susan stated.

As she poured the tea, she couldn't help but wonder why Delia chose to spend time with her. They were of different social circles, economic backgrounds, and even a good fifteen-year difference in age. Yet it was clear without saying it out loud that both women loved spending time with one another.

The same went for Mary. However, Mary was only a few years older than Susan.

"I just needed someone other than Brandon to talk to for a little while. I know that Mary doesn't like to leave the convent after eight PM."

Susan was essentially telling Delia that she really only had one friend to turn to.

Delia smiled. "You and I always end up having more fun without the nun anyway," Delia said as she sipped her tea.

It would bother Susan when someone would say something negative about Mary. Yes, she would defend Delia herself in a heartbeat, but Mary was a different story.

A lot of people were not fond of the nun for one reason or another. It seemed to be mostly because she could be seen as too holy sometimes, which Susan herself never saw. They rarely ever discussed the subject of religion.

Delia shook her head. "Oh, you want to tell me how Mary would be just as fun. You and I both know that she would just tell us to act our ages and behave," Delia pointed out.

Susan knew that she wasn't exactly lying about this, but it didn't change the fact that she always wanted to give Mary the benefit of the doubt. Being a nun who spent most of her free time with two women from rival families probably wasn't easy.

It had taken a few years, but Susan's mother finally put it together that maybe the Knight family were not the kind and caring group that Susan's father Seamus relentlessly made them out to be. She never told them that the only reason they even ended up with a good deal was because of herself and Delia forging paperwork.

Delia's husband Benton and late father-in-law Heathcliff were trying to trick the Fitzpatrick family into signing a deal that would have basically left them penniless, which at that time they essentially already were.

Mary had not been pleased that they went about doing things in the way they did. She felt they should have just gotten a lawyer involved. Susan, unfortunately, knew that was never going to be an option. Her father idolized the Knight family and still did even if he knew now that he probably would never have their respect.

The front door opened again, and shockingly it was Mary. She ran over but seemed to be in terror that Delia was there.

"What are you doing here?" the nun asked the socialite.

"Susan invited me, and my family was pissing me off," Delia explained as she took another sip of iced tea. "Non-alcoholic, in case you were wondering," Delia said as she held the glass up.

Mary sighed, "You know what, I should tell anyway."

She sat down next to Delia and looked around. "I was in the school part of Saint Agnes, and I heard a loud noise in the hallway. I went out to see what was going on, and your husband stormed out of the room," Mary admitted.

"Well, that explains why he was late to dinner."

Delia didn't really seem to be bothered by this.

"It gets worse. After he marched off, there was another man in the room he had been in. It was someone from the Costa organization," Mary told them.

Susan was a bit shocked by this. However, she had to admit she had met several Costas over the last few years. They were intimidating but far from the worst people she had ever dealt with.

"I need a refill!" screamed Mrs. Templeton.

Now that would be the worst person who she had probably ever dealt with.

Brandon came running out from the back with a glass

for the lovely lady. Maybe Susan was wrong about Nadia's belief that he was too into her. Maybe Brandon just enjoyed playing hero to women, which was a good thing for Susan in this instance. She knew that Nadia most definitely hated that, though.

"I mean, we really don't know what the meeting was about," Delia said.

Susan could tell that Delia was eyeing a bottle from behind the bar. She quickly moved in front of it.

Mary rubbed her forehead. "Delia! Susan! This is not a meeting between a Knight and some Ford executive. This is a meeting between the head of Knight Motor Company and the most notorious Michigan crime family," the nun reminded them both.

"I just don't think you should throw around the word notorious like that." Delia shrugged a bit.

HARRY – JUNE 2019

After dinner, the two boys sat on the back porch. Jackie had to go to the art gallery for a meeting, and Anthony was somewhere in the house doing work. What kind of work who knows? Harry knew it was best not to question that sort of stuff with the Costa family, which was bizarre, because out of everything, the mob aspect of the family was the one thing that didn't flair up his anxiety. It was just there.

"I don't think that went well on my end," he admitted out loud to his boyfriend.

Preston put his hand on his lap. "You did fine. You had no one to impress. My parents already adore you."

It was nice to know that his parents liked him. It was nice to know that his own parents were growing on to the idea of him and Preston together. Harry had no worries about his relationship, aside from the fact that he was always afraid that something would crumble.

It just didn't feel real that he had a near-perfect

boyfriend. Preston hated when he would say this. He insisted that he wasn't perfect. Harry didn't believe this, though. He knew damn well that Preston was perfect, at least in his mind.

Preston put up with him, and he hadn't abandoned him. That was more than any of the other people in his life; his mother twice, his aunt when his mother came back, Hannah, Hope, Brad twice, and Langley.

His father was consistent but at times distant. He knew that his father tried his damn hardest to be connected in his life, but there just wasn't much the two Knight men had in common. His father Cliff had been a basketball star at Saint Agnes with many friends.

Harry sat in the library most days when Preston was not available and before Preston was in his life.

Life as a Knight was always difficult for Harry. You didn't get the choice of which family you were born into. The question for Harry was, did he plan on staying a Knight once he did graduate at the end of the year?

"What are your plans for college?"

"Oh, lord... I'm not ready to think about that. I'm waiting until we get back to put together my list of schools.

Obviously, we will do it together," Preston responded.

Fuck... Harry had totally forgotten that there was a chance the two men wouldn't be going to the same college together. After all the loss in friendships he had, he wasn't about to do a long-distance relationship.

"I mean, I don't mind following you wherever you go." Harry explained.

The slick backed haired boy smiled and kissed his boyfriend.

"Harry, you have to do what is right for you. The school of your dreams could be out West for all we know."

"I highly doubt it. I'm not really looking to surround myself with a billion other people in a large city."

He knew that many gay people seemed to think that the big city was the way to go. It wasn't for him, though. New York sounded like anxiety as a visual. Chicago just seemed too green. LA and the likes were other big no's for him. He didn't need to stay in Grosse Pointe the rest of his life, though. He wouldn't mind Rochester Hills or West Bloomfield. Those were nice quiet areas.

"We have time to talk that all through," Preston said as

he cleared his throat. "So, then, any weekend plans before the big trip?"

Just repacking four hundred times.

"Nope. Probably just chill out at the house." He remembered Gena's offer for the party. He was pretty sure it was tomorrow. Harry really had no desire to go, but he knew that Preston would probably be into it.

"You know I was invited to this party."

His boyfriend's eyes widened. Why did he feel that the only reason he was looking at him like this was that he was shocked to hear that he, by himself, had been invited to a party?

"Just this person from the GSA. I don't know. Supposedly a few Saint Agnes kids will be there."

"Let's go!" Preston practically shouted. It sort of caught him off guard. "I mean, we can go, but yeah, I think we should. Just one last send-off before I take you into the unknown."

PRESTON – JUNE 2019

At the end of the day, Preston wasn't entirely sure why he said he wanted to go to this party. A few people from school had actually mentioned it, and it seemed to be just a typical get drunk party.

He knew damn well that Harry would react negatively to it. That said, he wanted to do something different than what they normally did. They normally watched TV, which consisted of romantic comedies on cable or something. Harry hated *Drag Race, Top Model,* and anything *Real Housewives*. He would even settle for daytime TV, but it made Harry overly anxious.

There were times when even he had to admit that Harry could be a little much. At times it felt as if there was something extra that was not being divulged to him specifically. It was hard to put a nail on what it could actually be, though, so he tried not to bring it up. At no point in his life had he ever thought he would be going on dates to the therapist's office to keep his boyfriend calm. Yet here he was. It didn't bother Preston. It just was not something he ever thought that he would be doing.

Drinking, loud music, the smell of tobacco and weed. This was a typical teenage party, not like the parties the two men usually ended up at, which were parties that adults threw to brag about themselves. A party like this existed because teenagers wanted to be just that. Teenagers.

At no point did Preston see himself ever conforming to those gala-type events that his parents went to. He remembered this year's Grosse Pointe General Hospital person of the year awards. It was absolutely dreadful. The only highlight of that evening was when Mrs. Templeton scooped up her ice cream with her bare hand and threw it at Harry's aunt Vivica. This was proceeded by her calling his aunt The Whore from Beverly Hills, which was the longstanding nickname that she had acquired back when she was a teenager.

This town was brutal. Preston grasped this. Harry was afraid of leaving it, though.

"I don't see Gena. I don't want people to think we snuck in," Harry said, frightened.

There were people here who looked to be college age and a few wearing lettermen jackets from schools in different counties.

Preston sighed, "I think we will be fine. I'm sure we will

see Gena at some point. Until then, just enjoy yourself."

Admittedly even Preston found the music a bit too loud. He wasn't sure if he would drink, although he knew that Harry wouldn't be. On occasion, he would have a cup of beer or something at a party when he actually got Harry to go out with him. He knew that his boyfriend wasn't that fond of him drinking. It freaked him out because they were underage. It wasn't like he was doing it often, though.

At times it did feel like Preston had inherited the problems of others with Harry. When Langley was around, Harry would go to her about things that bothered him. Specifically, things that freaked him out about his relationship with himself. Preston had a feeling that Harry went to Hannah on occasion, but more often than not, he found himself talking Harry out of his self-convinced thoughts that he wasn't right for him.

Preston genuinely liked Harry. There was something about him. He had to admit that Harry was hot. His eyes were just beyond belief. His curly messy hair was sexy. Harry would constantly say that Preston was the more attractive of the two. Preston disagreed a hundred percent on that.

"Oh, there she is!" Harry said. He grabbed hold of Preston's arm and took him over. "H-h-h-hi Gena!" He just barely got it out.

This Gena person was dark-skinned with blonde streaked hair. It shocked Preston to no end that Harry would interact with Gena. "Hi!" Gena said back.

They looked directly at Preston, "Oh my gosh! You are the famous Preston that Harry is always talking about. I can just tell. It has to be!"

Where on earth did Harry meet this person? They were overly happy, and Harry was ready to hide in a shell. Preston decided not to think so much about it.

"It's nice to finally meet you." He had maybe heard five words about them in the past.

"It's nice to meet you as well. Ok, so straight off the bat. Why don't you attend the GSA with Harry?" they asked.

That's the question everyone asked. If anything, Preston probably would have gotten more out of it than his boyfriend chose to get.

"I just have a million things to do." Which was true. He played football in the fall, tutored people in the winter, and did baseball and tutoring in the spring. That was at least the answer he gave everyone.

In reality, he probably could have shown up for meetings every once in a while. It wasn't like attendance was mandatory. There were just parts of him that he wasn't ready to share with people. He looked at Gena. They were living their best life. His parents were fine with whatever he chose. Preston wanted to believe that Harry would be as well. It was just the rest of the world he was still afraid of. People expected the football player to be masculine. Football players didn't play with dolls or have an interest in makeup.

The football teams' alumni group was already not fond of him being on the team because of his sexuality and the fact that he was a Costa. His father would just match every donation made whenever any sort of a vote would come up. The school and church were not in a position to not take the money.

"We would all love to have you at a meeting!" Gena smiled.

Harry was clearly frowning. "I don't even know if I will be at the meetings anymore. Owen sort of kind of told me that he didn't want me at them anymore."

Why would he say that? There were definitely times that Preston wanted to put duct tape on his boyfriend's mouth. Harry could go a month without saying a word, then he would scream something like that.

"Now, Harry, let's not say something without merit."

Why did he just sound like a parent saying that? He sounded like one of the nuns at Saint Agnes...

"Owen is honestly an asshole. A bunch of us are probably going to request a new adviser soon, to be honest. He's just looking for a few things to add to a resume," Gena admitted.

This was information that an average person would just nod about, however, Harry would spend the next month talking about this every chance he got.

"I mean, you know how older people are..."

Preston tried to swiftly change the subject. Harry shot him up a look, which was odd for Harry.

"He is in his twenties."

Ok, well, the guy was a jerk. The best thing for Harry still was to move past this. The last thing that he needed was for Harry to spend their vacation going insane over Owen being an asshole. He'd get his father or uncle involved if that is the case, and things wouldn't end well for anyone if he actually had to get involved.

"It's a great party." Preston once again tried to change the subject.

Gena nodded and smiled, "Thanks! I have to mingle a bit around, but I definitely want to hang out a little more before the end of the night. Enjoy yourselves!" they said as they walked into the crowd to greet people.

Gena definitely was on their way to being a new age socialite of the town.

In Preston's opinion, they at least seemed nice, unlike some of the town's socialites, such as Margot Fitzpatrick, a stuck-up family friend of his parents and the aunt of Harry's cousin Brad. That woman was just ruthless and insane.

Then, of course, there was Mrs. Templeton, the town bigot with a creepy ice cream obsession. No one was really sure of how old she was. Harry had once shown him a picture of his great-grandparents standing next to her at a very young age. She looked older in that picture than she did at her current age.

Gena might have a chance at changing the landmark of Grosse Pointe if they chose to stick around.

Preston often wondered if things could turn a new leaf for this upper crest old town. He liked to think that people were capable of evolving. Grosse Pointe was just a weird place.

The Italian had no real issues with where he lived. It was just that he wanted to venture into new adventures, which is when he again looked at his boyfriend. This trip was going to be an adventure...

"I don't... I don't... I don't think I feel well," Harry explained, looking at him. This wasn't their first rodeo.

Preston grabbed Harry and held him in the middle of the crowd. This made him feel as uncomfortable as Harry usually felt. This party might have been hosted by a queer person, but that didn't mean that assholes weren't bound to show up at some point.

Harry broke from the hug. "Preston! We are in public."

It was sad, but Preston knew that Harry was way too freaked out by PDA.

"It's ok, Harry. Let's get out of here."

Honestly, it would have been great to spend a little more time here. It was nice to go somewhere with Harry.

Preston just had to keep reminding himself that things were going to be exciting next week. He just had to keep reminding himself of this.

HARRY – JUNE 2019

I have everything, right? Everything seems to be here. I know that I have my luggage all ready, but do I need all this stuff? Maybe I need more. Preston is going to freak out when he sees that I'm bringing three bags. One is a backpack, and it has my laptop. Do I need my laptop? I have stuff to do for fall. He knows that. I mean, really, it isn't like I'm not going to be home in a week. Fuck... I wish Preston would just tell me where the fuck we are going. Why am I swearing so much?

The Knight teen looked at his three bags and sighed. He needed to repack one more time. The sun was just starting to rise. He had been up all night trying to figure this out.

Someone knocked on the door. He assumed it was going to be Preston surprising him early. He quickly threw one of the bags on the side of his bed, realizing it was the one with his laptop in it.

"Come in!" Harry screamed. He had no idea why he just started to scream. It was just Hannah. She was still in her robe.

"Harry, are you alright?" She rubbed her eyes for a moment. "I've been hearing noises in here all night. I normally wouldn't ponder, but lord, I need some sleep."

She sat on his bed and looked at the bags.

"Harry, it's a weeklong trip. You aren't going to need half of this."

The brother dropped himself on the bed and laid next to his sister.

"I have no idea what I'm doing."

Hannah sighed, "Men have no idea how to pack for things. Actually, no, let me correct that. Straight men pack a change of socks but not a change of underwear. That's it. Gay men bring their entire closet with them.

I remember when I was living with those loser roommates. One of the guys went on a trip with a new boyfriend, and they had to rent a van because they pretty much packed up their rooms. You will be gone for a week. You can wear the same pair of pants more than once but get multiple shirt options. Plus, underwear. Especially if you are going to share a bed with him."

This mortified him. "Why on earth would I worry about

underwear in bed?"

"I suppose those are optional," Hannah laughed.

That wasn't at all what he meant.

"Do you want to maybe come along with us?"

She started to laugh again, "Stop overthinking all of this. You need to stay calm. I'm also going to suggest keeping your phone off. The last thing you need is a hundred messages from dad and aunt Vivica freaking out that you are not feeling safe."

He already knew that his parents were going to text him nonstop. They would text him in the morning, afternoon, and evening.

"I don't want them worrying. I'm sure they keep a tracking device on me."

His sister sort of shrugged at this. "I have no idea." She looked off into the distance.

***

Harry took a deep breath in the North Pointe foyer. He opened the door, and Preston was standing outside with a smile. He was wearing a black t-shirt and tan shorts. He looked really sexy in shorts, especially with his athletic legs. The Knight boy could look at his boyfriend for hours on end without saying anything. There were times that he really wished that were a possibility. It would avoid so many crazy conversations.

"Hi," he hardly muttered out.

The Costa teen smiled, "Hello, Mr. Knight. I'm here to scoop you away for a weeklong secret getaway. Are you ready?"

"No," Harry said nervously out loud. The two boys looked at each other and laughed. Preston grabbed him by the waist and kissed him on the lips. Harry broke from the kiss.

"Are you sure you are ready to put up with me for a weeklong journey?"

"I'm ready to put up with you for a lifelong journey Mr. Knight."

He winked and walked into North Pointe. He grabbed two of Harry's bags. Harry was wearing his backpack at the moment.

"I'm shocked that there are only three bags."

Hannah had tried to convince Harry that he didn't need half the things, but half the things were actual essential items.

"It's all very important stuff. I swear!"

The two boys made their way outside and down the path to Preston's car. They put the bags in the trunk. Preston's own bag was back there. It consisted of just his backpack.

Harry looked around. He looked behind him at his aunt's abandoned mansion across the street. He then turned and saw Mrs. Templeton's unkept front lawn with the Aunt Jemima figure that Holly had been fighting with the city to have removed for over a year.

He then looked right in front of him at the haunting home that was North Pointe. He couldn't help but smile at the thought of getting away, after all that had happened over the past year.

The boy nonchalantly waved goodbye as he got into the passenger seat.

"Alright, Mr. Knight, let's get the hell out of Grosse Pointe!" Preston said as he floored it out of the driveway jokingly.

He slowed down a bit once they got on the street. "Any guesses as to where we are going?"

"Camping?" Harry suggested.

Preston turned to him and gave him a look of disbelief. "Do either of us look like we could survive in the wild?"

If he were being honest, he assumed that Preston could. He knew the answer was not the same for himself, though.

"Are we staying in the state?"

This, for some reason, made his boyfriend laugh.

"Eh... no. We are going to be leaving the state. Don't worry, I've already given all the information to Hannah, Holly, your aunt, and dad, plus, my own parents. Everyone but you knows where we are going."

He smiled at this. It sort of annoyed Harry that every member of his family knew where they were going, but he didn't.

It was a long shot, but Harry decided that this would be the perfect time to shoot Langley a text message. It was unlikely that she would even read it,

but he wanted her to know that he was leaving and that he missed her. He quickly sent it. He also sent one to Brad. He knew that Brad would probably at least read it but never find the words to respond.

Harry just wanted things to go back to normal. Yet, at the same time, he was admittedly happy with his new life. He had Preston. He was finally close with Hannah. His aunt and father were finally married.

Heck, even after last night, he felt like he might have a friend in Gena. The world was changing around him. He didn't like change, and yet at this moment, he was actually ok with it for once. Sort of, but not really, but it was ok.

The two boys passed the Ford Mansion. It would just be a moment now, and they would be out of Grosse Pointe. It would actually be a good thing to get out of Grosse Pointe, Harry had to admit to himself. Five... Four... Three... Two... One...

"So, I'm going to make a few detours before we get on the highway. We should probably stop for some snacks as we will be on the freeway for a while," Preston explained to him.

These detours were code for Harry to use the damn restroom while we are still on the main roads because I'm not stopping when we get on the freeway. Preston knew Harry very well at this point.

"Obviously, we will stop for the night when it gets dark, or I get tired."

Harry smiled, "I could always drive a little bit just pointing out."

"Oh, don't worry, you will once we get to the final destination. You will also drive on the way back, but I don't want to give away the surprise at all. So, nope no driving for you just yet," the mobster's son explained.

The Knight boy knew that they definitely were not on their way to Canada since Preston didn't instruct him to take his passport with him. At the same time, that wasn't completely out of the question either. For all Harry knew, his passport was in the glove compartment.

All of a sudden, it just dawned on Harry, "This isn't your car."

The straight-haired teen laughed, "Good eye. No. I rented this one for the week. Your car is still in the shop, and my parents didn't want me to take my car with my license plate for safety issues."

"I mean Preston, I can get you a deal on a Knight car. As in, basically take any vehicle off the lot of any Knight dealership with basically no paperwork. You do realize that?"

The only reason that Harry was adamant about getting his car back in shape instead of getting a new one was that he knew that car. It made him feel comfortable driving instead of another model or even the same model where it would feel different. It just would be. It was hard to explain, but it wouldn't be the same.

The Italian boy just shrugged, "I mean, it doesn't really matter now. I just didn't want to get into details over the situation."

This was always a weird subject when it came to things that involved his parents. Sometimes Harry wished he was brave enough to ask Preston about the real dangers that came from the Costa family. Yet, at the same time, the ignorance is bliss approach also worked very well for him. He knew that the skeletons

in the Costa family closet were much worse than he probably needed to know.

It wasn't as if the Knight family had a squeaky-clean reputation. They just had the best PR team that money could buy.

His great-grandfather was shot in the foyer of North Pointe. His grandfather, it seemed, slept with every woman in town throughout his life, and was top guy responsible for the deaths of more than a few people. His father, Cliff, ran over someone back in the early 2000s. It was ruled an accident, but who knows if that was true or not. His aunt Vivica was known as the Whore from Beverly Hills, on top of being a serial bride until her recent marriage to his father. It was their first legal marriage. Harry himself didn't even have a clean image anymore, in a very small way, because he was dating Preston. Harry wouldn't change that part for anything.

The young couple continued to drive. Eventually, they drove out of Saint Clair Shores and Roseville.

"We are now entering Warren, Michigan. If you look on your right, you will be able to see elderly people chain-smoking as they feed squirrels," Preston joked.

They drove a little more before he drove into the parking lot of a Jordon Food Store.

"Why are we stopping here?" Harry asked.

"Remember? I told you we were going to stop to stock up on snacks," Preston pointed out.

That part he remembered, "I just thought you meant like a gas station."

His boyfriend shrugged, "It's a bulk grocery store. We can get a lot. This way, we don't have to stop. Remember, I don't want to be on the freeway forever. The quicker we get to our destination, the better."

"Hannah used to work at a Jordon Food Store. They didn't treat her very well," Harry pointed out.

"She mentioned that once. That was the Royal Oak location Harry. This is the Warren location. Different locations have different employees." There was a point in this statement. It still wouldn't have been Harry's first choice, but he guessed that it was a better option than a gas station.

As they walked into the store, their body temperatures both dropped. It was scorching hot outside and freezing inside.

"Wow, there are no carts in here," Preston pointed out. He looked over at the register and saw one behind a giant bin of boxes. He walked over and said hello to the cashier.

She was busy stabbing a box with a small knife.

"Hi, do you mind if I take this cart?" He waited for a response, but she said nothing.

"Hello?" he spoke. No response.

Preston waited another moment, but then he just took the cart. This seemed to finally trigger the cashier.

"Hold your horses there, mister. I... I... I uh... uh... um... I need that cart. You see, I was using it for... for stuff," the short woman said.

This woman was clearly slurring her words. Harry gestured for Preston to walk over to him so he wouldn't be alone. He didn't like going into places alone, and it felt weird to be away from Preston, even if only about twenty feet or so away. "What on earth was that?" he asked.

"I don't know...maybe she is tired?" Preston suggested.

As they ventured down the first aisle, they grabbed a pack of sports drinks for the road. Preston made a point to explain to Harry that he didn't need to binge drink them and then make them stop halfway through the freeway. There was nothing they needed down the second aisle, and the third aisle seemed to be where the snacks were.

It was then that Harry noticed that they were the only other customers in the store, it seemed. Yet again, there were no carts in the cart area when they had entered the building.

"This place is pretty dead," Harry said out loud.

"I noticed that too. Aside from that cashier, I don't think I've seen any other employees either. It's not that I need to ask any questions. It just seems odd that the only person you have on the floor is someone who clearly isn't completely there," Preston pointed out.

This was completely true. It felt like they could easily get away with shoplifting, which was something that Harry would never do. He wondered if Preston would. He doubted it. Could Preston shoplift? It seemed like something that a Costa would do. Why was he thinking such things? This was his boyfriend.

He shouldn't be thinking that way about his boyfriend. It would definitely be easy to get past that crazy woman upfront. Still, she couldn't possibly be the only person in the store. Could she be? Harry really hoped not.

"Do we get the brand name chips or the JFS brand chips? The JFS chips are bigger," Preston pointed out.

"Brand name! I don't trust off-brand," Harry said with a touch of a snob in his voice. This sort of made Preston give him a look, but Harry didn't seem to notice.

The boyfriend put the brand-name chips in the cart and continued onward. There were giant bags of popcorn that were almost as tall as the two of them. Well… down to their waists. They were both over six feet tall.

"I wonder why they would put pots and pans down the same aisle as the chips and candy?"

"I'm wondering why they randomly have the Hispanic and Asian food in a small corner with the rest of the food," Harry pointed out.

They bypassed the next few aisles because they were all paper goods. They were now in what appeared to be the dairy, meat, and produce area. It was sort of a mess, as in nothing was in a likeminded place, and nothing looked like it had been cleaned in a few weeks—the onion peels were all over the fruit. Preston reluctantly grabbed a thing of bagged apples.

"Why don't we grab some of those bagged salads for right now?" Preston suggested.

This sounded like a good idea for lunch, so Harry went

over and looked through the selection. There was a Caesar salad kit that looked somewhat appealing. However, upon checking the expiration date, Harry noticed that it had gone bad a week ago. He quickly went through a few bags, and the best date was for the next day, but it looked to be in worse shape than the one that had definitely expired. He walked right back over to Preston.

"I don't think we can eat those."

Preston sighed. He walked back over. It was obvious that Preston thought that Harry was being picky again. The Italian boy looked at the bag, and his eyes widened.

"Ok then, let's skip out on the salad."

"Also, the yogurt," Harry pointed out as he quickly slammed that door shut. The boyfriends looked at one another and decided that they would get what they had in the cart and then get the heck out of the store. There were a few fast-food places on the way up the highway they could stop at really quickly.

As they got into the line, the cashier was still sort of out of it. "Hi, we just wanted to buy these items," Preston explained to her.

It took her a minute to process things. She looked at the

ceiling. Harry didn't mean to, but he looked up himself. Preston suddenly stopped him. The cashier, whose name was Juanita, started to scan the items. She tried to lift the twenty-four-pack of sports drink but had difficulty. Preston tried to help her, but this only seemed to agitate her. He very quickly stepped back for her to continue whatever the heck it was she was doing.

They had like five items, and yet it felt she was ringing up four carts of groceries with how long she was taking. A line started to form. There had been no one else in the store five minutes ago and yet now... Harry had to think for a moment, that there was someone else in the store. Yet, she was clearly not going to call for backup.

It was at this point that she was finally done. This was where things got a bit weird. There was a woman wearing some tan jeans and an almost see-through white blouse in her late forties, who started to scratch herself. The two boyfriends looked at one another as she reached down and started to scratch her crotch area. At this point, she took her other hand and reached for a tuna sandwich that had been hiding under the register, which was open the entire time.

Juanita looked at them, "Oh, sorry, where are my manors? You guys want a bite?"

She switched hands and now was holding the sandwich she had just gone down on herself with.

Harry whipped out his wallet and threw out two hundred dollars. The price was only around forty-something dollars. He grabbed the cart, and they both ran out of the store.

"Wait! Damn it, now my register is going to be over again," Juanita thought for a moment. "Actually, nope. It's still going to be under. I forgot to take cash a few times earlier."

The two teens ran into the parking lot over to the rented Knight vehicle. They looked at one another and started laughing hysterically.

"How the hell did Hannah work there?"

"I don't know, but she did it for three years," Harry pointed out.

Saying that out loud made him sad. That was three years where she must have dealt with similar things on a daily basis. She could have lived at home during that era, but she stayed away.

He knew why. Their mother, Tiffany Weston-Knight,

was not welcoming to her. She just wasn't very motherly to either of them. She always got along with their sister Hope, but for whatever reason, she couldn't figure out how to bond with either him or Hannah. It made him sad to think that she would choose to live in a crowded house with roommates over North Pointe, all while working here of all places.

MARY – JUNE 1968

The whole conversation the night before had been pointless. The nun asked the strawberry blonde to meet her at the Harbor Inn the next day, and she did.

"Thank goodness you finally showed up." Mary practically spat out her drink.

Susan sat and looked confused. "Look, I understand being a bit freaked about the concept of running into Benton and someone from the Costa family, but Mary, you don't even like Benton Knight," Susan pointed out.

Even though she wanted to say that it was a sin to hate, Susan didn't say hate; she said she "didn't like", which was very much true. She didn't like Benton Knight. She also essentially hated Benton Knight, but she wouldn't say that out loud.

"Even if I do dislike Benton Knight, that doesn't mean that I shouldn't worry about my friend's wellbeing," Mary explained as she crossed her arms.

The Fitzpatrick daughter looked around, "Look, the Costa family have been working with my father for a few months. I didn't want to say anything because they are doing legitimate business from what my father says," Susan told the nun.

Mary couldn't believe what Susan just nonchalantly stated. "You honestly trust him?" Mary asked.

Her friend brushed her hair back. "Oh goodness no. But I also know that my father is not known for making great choices."

The nun was more than aware of this. The Fitzpatrick parents were known throughout the town for not being the brightest people. They chased ideas and not realities.

"I'm just worried about Delia's safety, and now I guess your own," Mary admitted. She looked down at the menu for a moment.

Susan shuffled around a bit in her seat. "I appreciate that you are concerned. Really, I am. I've just learned to live with certain things as time goes on," the strawberry blonde explained.

Mary could sense that there was more to that statement than she was saying.

"What else have you had to live with?" she asked.

Susan looked out the window. "Oh… um, nothing really. Just stuff," she claimed.

Mary knew that she was holding something in. "You can tell me anything, Susan. We've been friends for several years now. If anything, you are probably my best friend."

Mary smiled. It was as if Susan wanted to say something, but she wouldn't allow herself to say it.

"Mary… I…" She was interrupted by someone walking in the front entrance. It was Rodrick Knight with Nadia Bloom? That made no sense.

Nadia clearly saw the two of them and walked over.

"I'm having lunch with Rodrick. Why? He harassed me for twenty minutes in the parking lot. That's why," the teenage girl explained. She looked pissed off.

"Would you prefer to sit with us?" Susan asked.

Nadia looked over at Rodrick, who had this smirk on his face.

"Yes… Scooch over," she said, a little rude in tone.

DELIA – JUNE 1968

The current family matriarch sat down at the kitchen table. Her husband was already sitting reading the daily paper. They rarely spent time together outside of the bedroom as of late, and it wasn't as if they spent that time doing anything other than sleep.

"So, I heard you ran into Mary last night," she stated to him.

Benton sighed and put the paper down. "When we got married, you agreed you didn't want to know how I conducted my business. You said you found it boring," her husband reminded her.

That was true. It was very boring. Benton tended to brag about the most mundane things possible. However, this mostly applied to when they lived out in California when they first got married, when he had an office job.

At the beginning of their marriage, what a difference. Things were fine up until they moved to Michigan. Benton had moved out to California to work for the west coast division of KMC after college. It was an excuse to escape both of his parents. His mother begged and pleaded with him to return when she became ill years later. They had only ventured out to Michigan for holidays until that point, which Delia had been fine with.

It was nice to have what Benton called an authentic Christmas with snow and all the trimmings instead of what California called Christmas.

However, Heathcliff and Jenny Knight were not fond of Delia. She could also tell that there was resentment that their children were Hispanic.

Rodrick had slightly paler skin and Knight blonde hair. However, Clifton was darker and definitely had a Latin spark to him, which was probably why Heathcliff had warmed up to Rodrick so much in his final years.

It was realizing this that once again made her feel eternal guilt over Clifton running off to Europe with his now teenage wife, Dallas. Not only did Delia disapprove of Dallas, but his grandfather disapproved of his heritage. Why would he have wanted to stick around?

"Do you think of Clifton often?"

Delia turned and looked at her husband. Benton turned

to her for a brief moment. "What?" he essentially snapped at her.

"I just miss our son more and more as of late," Delia sighed.

She wanted to sink to the floor but knew that was not appropriate. She could tell that Benton was about to say something of prominence when the backdoor opened...

"Your little friends decided to interrupt my chance with a girl this afternoon," Rodrick spat at her as he ran upstairs.

PRESTON – JUNE 2019

It had been three hours on the road. So, far they were making good time. Preston had a good feeling that it would only take around a day to get to their destination.

Harry was wearing headphones right now, listening to some sort of music; more than likely, Taylor Swift or a boyband.

In Preston's mind, Harry had no flaws regardless of his mental state of mind. However, if he were forced to name a singular flaw in the curly-haired teen, it would be that Harry had some terrible taste in music. No indie. No classics. There was nothing wrong with the top 100. It was just that he never tried to venture out of that.

It was the same with his taste in movies. They watched blockbusters and comedies—no foreign films and no awards contenders, even though Preston knew most awarded films were never the best films of the year. He had tried to get Harry to watch the films of Fellini or even a few French-language films. Harry just got very squeamish about them. He did not like black and white films, and for whatever reason, Italian seemed to freak him out. He did, however, enjoy it when Preston would call him beautiful and amazing in Italian.

The Italian boy was bilingual. His whole family was minus his mother. However, Jackie definitely knew what was being said. She just didn't speak the language, so it was impossible to get anything by her. His father insisted that it was an important skill that he and his sister know more than one language. It would look good on a college application.

Obviously, his father did not want either of his children to enter the family business. If Anthony did, he didn't show it because Jackie most definitely was not about to let one of her children be in the mob, even though when you were born into the mob, you were always going to be a target. Preston knew this all too well.

He could be a schoolteacher in Wisconsin, but there would always be a bullet on him if something happened to Anthony or someone else within the organization. There were things in place if his father was ever shot. It was morbid to think about the fact that his father had this conversation with him when he started eighth grade, but at this point, it was just a part of his life.

It worried him beyond belief to think about what would

happen if he and Harry got married. Could they live a normal life? Obviously not considering Harry himself was a Knight, which in itself was an issue for them.

It was cliché to say out loud, but the reality was that they were sort of star-crossed lovers. Preston's parents liked Harry. Harry's father and aunt definitely had come around a lot more in recent months to accept that he was with Harry. However, the two families still hated one another. His aunt had excellent reasons. Her ex-husband had switched her own child Brad, with a baby that had miscarried and gave him to Anthony to raise. This was after Jackie ran off with Preston after having a brief moment of not wanting Anthony to raise a child. She came back after six or so months, but Vivica spent that time mourning a child that was living across the street from her.

There was no doubt in his mind that kids in Grosse Pointe grew up way too fast. In Preston's case, it felt like he was only eight years old just a year ago, and now he was a year away from graduating high school. It was as if there was something in the water source or something.

Harry took his headphones off. He was looking at his phone.

"I just got my final grades emailed. I apparently did well in every subject but gym. How on earth could I get a

C in gym?"

"Harry, you don't really participate in gym," Preston pointed out.

This made his boyfriend sigh loudly, "I give it my all. We can't all be built like you!"

It was very hard to tell if Harry meant this as a compliment or an insult.

"I mean, I've always been fond of your body." Harry had a toned but very thin physique which Preston found to be very sexy. Preston found everything about Harry to be sexy.

"I guess I'm in shape. I just wish I were as muscular as you are," Harry explained.

Something about that made him cringe. It was a nice compliment, but Preston had some body image issues that he had been working on as of late.

"How would you feel if I shaved my legs?" Preston sort of slipped out on purpose.

His boyfriend turned to him, "Shave your legs? Why?"

"I've never really been fond of hair on my body aside from my head," he admitted.

"I guess it's not something I've ever thought of one way or the other about you. Your eyes and smile have always been the highlight of your features. Your personality is what makes my heart melt, though," Harry explained.

Preston couldn't help but have his own heart melt a bit from this statement. There were definitely times that he wondered if Harry was more physically than emotionally attracted to him. It was nice to know that it was indeed his personality that turned him on. It made him more comfortable.

"How would you feel if I started to wear a little makeup? Just a little?" He prepositioned this as a slight joke.

It was sort of obvious that this took Harry back a bit. "Um, if you really wanted, but your skin is always so clear. Why would you need to cover it with anything?"

That wasn't the reason he wanted to wear makeup. He wanted to wear it as a form of expression. There were so many cool looks that he would see on the internet from other guys and non-conforming individuals that made him so jealous that they had those skills.

"So, what you are saying is that you wouldn't take issue with it?"

"I'm not going to stop you from doing anything," Harry shrugged as he put his headphones back on. He turned them up a bit. Good lord, he was still listening to Taylor Swift.

This was a step in the right direction and one of the reasons he had insisted on taking Harry to their final destination. Preston just wanted to feel comfortable in his own skin, but in part, that meant making sure that Harry would be comfortable with that. It just made him so nervous.

As of late, there were mornings when he would wake up and get out of bed, but he didn't feel like a he; he was a she. Then by the time Preston got out of the shower, he was back to feeling male. It was the most bizarre thing in the world.

His parents were supportive and trying to help him through his being confused about his identity. However, there was an issue that his father was mobster Anthony Costa and his mother was sort of a nut. He loved her with all his heart, but she was brash and abrasive in her own love. A very momma bear attitude that sometimes would go ten steps farther than they needed to go.

It was hard to say who had it worse, Preston as her son or Anthony as her husband. No woman dares to look Anthony Costa in the eye unless they want to face her wrath. She had his uncle Jack on her side, which only made it ten times scarier to think about.

Still, it was a step in the right direction in terms of his own confidence to know that Harry seemed to not really care one way or the other about him wearing makeup. Obviously, there was still context that needed to be explained.

HARRY – JUNE 2019

Why on earth was his boyfriend asking if he was ok with him wearing makeup? It wasn't something that he ever thought that he would hear Preston say. First, the dolls which threw him for a loop and now makeup?

There was something off about Preston as of late. Harry just couldn't figure out what it was exactly. At the same time, he realized they had been dating for a while now, and it only made sense that the two of them would become much more comfortable with asking one another these sorts of things.

This made him wonder if he should be asking the same questions to him. Could he handle the fact that his brain just didn't operate the way that most people did? There were times when he wanted to tell Preston he loved him and wanted to be with him for the rest of his life. He knew it was too soon to be thinking that way, but he couldn't help it.

This was just a natural reaction to young love and

being in a relationship with a normal person. Harry knew, though, deep down, that while it might have been normal there were times when his brain amplified those feelings past ten or even twenty.

It was hard to pinpoint when these emotions started. Surely, he must have been born this way. Yet, at the same time, it made sense that he would love hard and fear abandonment twice as hard. His mother disappeared when he was only a year old. He has no early memories of his mother, Tiffany. Then all of a sudden, she comes into his life, and his aunt Vivica and cousin Brad are gone from his life. Not only are they gone, but Brad isn't a few streets away. He is miles and miles away at boarding school.

His mother had not been very maternal. When he would act up, she would send him to his room, or on occasion, she would just leave because she couldn't handle it.

When it came to both him and Hannah, the go-to was always to point out how easy things came to Hope. *You need to be more like Hope. Hope can get straight A's. Hope is a cheerleader. Hope has all these friends. Why don't you have friends over? I planned a birthday for you, and no one showed up, Harry! Why on earth would you have me throw you this large party and no one show up?*

He quickly turned up the music. This wasn't what he

needed right now..., and all of a sudden, he sort of slipped into the past...

HARRY – MAY 2011

"Are we going to the zoo soon?" Harry asked his Aunt.

He jumped into her arms. His Aunt seemed off for some reason.

"Aunt Vivica, have you been crying?" the young boy asked her.

His Aunt wiped her tears, "Yes, darling, but they are happy tears." This confused him. He had never heard of happy tears.

"Why would you want to cry if you are happy. You should smile. Like this!" He made this giant toothy smile. This made his aunt laugh. He gave her a tight hug. "I love you, Aunt Vivica!"

She took him by the arms and looked him right in the eyes.

"I will always love you. You always need to remember

that Harry. I love you and your sisters very much. Regardless of what the world might throw our way, we are always going to be a family," she nodded, and he nodded back.

"So, is Brad getting ready for the zoo?" Harry wondered.

Vivica laughed. "Brad is actually visiting his Aunt Margot today," she explained. There was a tense tone in her saying this.

Harry was not fond of Brad's Aunt Margot. She tended to make his own Aunt not seem happy, which Harry did not like. She was sort of a mean lady.

"So, we aren't going to the zoo today?"

His Aunt shook her head, "No. Other things need to be done today. Harry, do you know your mommy?"

He thought about it for a moment. "I remember she was a pretty lady and a doctor."

"Yes, she is a doctor." In the context of the present, Harry realized now that his aunt avoided calling his mother pretty, which was sort of funny in context.

"Do you remember when you used to ask about why

she wasn't around?" His aunt asked him.

"You and dad used to tell me it was because she had to go away," Harry had explained.

Vivica smiled, "Yes, well... Harry, you are a very lucky boy. You see, unlike other people when their parents go away, they don't come back. Your mother is in a different situation. She has come back."

SUSAN – JUNE 1968

"It's going to be beautiful once it is complete!" Ida said as she hugged Seamus.

Susan couldn't help but smile for her parents. She agreed to meet them at the grounds of the home they had been building for several years now.

Brandon looked at her, and she could tell he thought the same thing. This house was never going to be done.

She just shrugged as a silent response.

Instead of putting the money from the family business into something that would help expand, their father decided to build a home that would equate to that of North Pointe. They were able to secure the land relatively cheaply. There was a fire on the original property from a mob war. They were on a street initially infested with prominent mob families. The only ones left were the Costa family, which, thinking of that now, was not lost on Susan.

She understood where Mary was coming from. She

really did. It was just pointless to argue with her father about business deals.

Had she not gotten herself involved, her father would have gladly taken the lousy deal that was originally presented to him from the Knight family. They would have been even poorer than before, but her father would have taken it as grounds to celebrate. He really would have, which was the scary part. Their luck really had changed.

"Well, if it isn't my soon-to-be neighbors," Luca Costa said as he walked up to the house from across the street.

He was a man probably around the same age as her own father. He was old, probably not in top shape, and was first-generation Italian American.

As the rumor had it, his father forced his mother to hold him in until they got off the boat on Ellis Island. However, he spoke with a slight Italian dialect, unlike her own Irish immigrant parents. It was herself and Brandon who were first-generation Irish American.

Seamus and Ida, of course, ran over and hugged the man. Was it because they were genuinely happy to see him or because he was a known kingpin? If Susan honestly had to guess, she would go with a valid third option; her father liked that he had power, which probably was sadly true.

"Oh, Luca, it is nice to see you today," Seamus said confidently.

The Fitzpatrick daughter was not exactly fond of how her father called the man by his first name. It showed that he didn't fear him, which might have been a negative and not a positive for them.

"How much longer until we can officially call one another neighbors?" the Costa man asked.

Brandon made himself front and center. "Probably another year at this rate," he said. Brandon said this in a tone that made Susan realize he was just as reluctant towards this as she was. Yet his body language said differently.

"I'd love to have you all over for dinner again soon," Luca stated to them.

He had a smile that was definitely on the charming side. If you didn't know who he was, you would probably be enchanted by him. Susan knew who he was, though, and that was where the problem remained.

"Oh, we most certainly would love to join you, your wife as well. Is she back from New York yet?" Seamus asked, a little too eager at the invitation, which annoyed Susan.

He always said yes to everything. Even she knew how to play coy, and she wasn't a businessperson.

"No. Not yet. Her sister is sick. It might be some time. But you are all always welcome in our home."

Luca looked at Susan. "My son, Sergio, was just talking about you the other day. He'd hate me for saying this to you, but I think he would enjoy spending some time with you," Luca stated.

This made Susan cringe. It always made her cringe when people tried to set her up on dates. Delia constantly tried to do so with people from her world. She thought that it would ease up Benton a little bit.

"Well... I mean, he is always free to come around the bar."

She had no idea why she just said that, probably not to offend the powerful man.

HARRY – JUNE 2019

This was very confusing for him at the time. He was too young to really understand the concept of death. He knew that death meant you didn't come back, but he didn't know that it meant you were no longer on this earth. It had struck a large chord for him at the time to think that his mother had, in a sense, abandoned him because that was what he believed to be the case.

Tiffany Knight had left him. In a sense, it made him feel like he had not been wanted by his mother. It didn't help that when she returned, she didn't know how to handle him. There was this disconnect between them. She didn't feel like his mother, nor did it seem that she wanted to go through the process of being his mother, yet he was kept from his aunt for so many years.

This was the era of time in which his father had also become distant. He had to deal with Hope's many achievements and Hannah always getting into trouble. He was left alone. On rare occasions when he was allowed to see his aunt, she always focused the entire time on him or him and his sisters.

Obviously, his aunt gave up a lot to make her sister that she didn't particularly like happy.

The town projected an unfair view onto her because she had been married to Nial Fitzpatrick. A lot of the unflattering views came from his own grandfather Rodrick. He remembered Rodrick from his youth. He had not been a very nurturing grandparent.

He really didn't remember his aunt and mother's own mother as he was very young when she died. His father, Cliff's mother, had supposedly abandoned him herself when he was a teenager. He had another grandfather that raised his mother Tiffany by himself in Beverly Hills. Every couple of years, he would show up out of nowhere and act a fool, usually at his aunt's expense. He was now a retired entertainment lawyer who dated much younger women. The guy was at least pleasant towards all of his grandchildren when he was around.

His family dynamic was very weird. The Knight family was just too visible to hide from. The Weston name was also too visible to hide from, thanks to his aunt.

There were times when he questioned if his father enjoyed the life that he had been given. It made Harry sad, though, to think about this.

All of a sudden, Harry's headphones died on him. He looked up, and it was pitch black outside. The Knight boy hadn't realized that he had been in his head that long. He turned to Preston, "Are we making good time?"

The Italian boy yawned. "I believe we are. It is getting late, though."

"I could drive a little bit. I'm just saying," Harry pointed out.

"Oh no, Mr. Knight. I will be doing the driving, at least until we get there. That said, I think we should stop for the night," Preston explained to him.

This seemed like a logical thing to do. At this moment, Harry realized this would be the first time they slept in the same bed together. If they got a single bed, that was. It was possible that Preston would get two beds instead of one. What on earth would it mean if he did this? Would it mean that he wasn't interested in being close with Harry? Did Harry want to be close with Preston in that way right now? It wasn't even a question of whether they would be having sex. It was a question of would they be in bed wearing less than they are now together. On occasion, they would cuddle together in bed, but they were always fully clothed and above the blanket. On the off chance that someone walked in, he didn't want anyone thinking anything. Preston never seemed to have an issue with this, which might be a telling sign. Did Preston choose that because he didn't want to get close to him sexually?

Harry, get out of your head, damn it! If I don't want to have sex with Preston tonight, then I won't. If he has an issue with that, then oh well. That doesn't mean I don't want to have sex with him, though. Once again... get out of my head.

It would be another ten minutes of driving and then getting off the freeway for them to find a hotel for the night.

It was some semi-nice chain hotel. Would it have been Harry's first choice personally? Probably not. However, it appeared to be the nicest out of all the ones in the same area based on the reviews they quickly looked up.

The lobby of the hotel seemed pretty standard. It wasn't something that you would lounge around in, although he was sure that some middle-class people trying to feel fancy probably did. Harry didn't even like lounging at nice hotels. The concept of being around strangers always freaked him out. The desk woman seemed like she had been up all day and was ready for bed herself.

He and Preston got into an elevator together, and when the door closed, Preston took his hand.

"We are about to be in a hotel room together. I just sort of realized that." He started to blush. It was a total turn-on.

"Yeah... I realized that a little bit ago," Harry said. He left it at that. The elevator doors opened. They were staying on the third floor. It seemed like every chain hotel had the same layout regardless if it was the same brand or not. The hallway had an ugly grey outline with red stripes on both sides. The walls had a cream-colored wallpaper with a rough texture to them.

Their room was at the end of the hallway. It was close to a fire exit, which calmed Harry a bit and freaked him out a bit. What would happen if there was a fire? Why would there be a fire? You couldn't smoke in hotel rooms anymore. That wouldn't stop people, though. At least Harry didn't think that it would. He had no idea, and he needed to stop thinking about it.

Preston opened the door and once again a very typical-looking hotel room. It was a bit nicer than normal, but not really. It was, of course, obnoxiously cold.

He peaked into the bathroom, and it was actually a nice layout. The signature tacky-looking teal blanket was on the queen-sized bed - queen-sized bed. They were indeed going to be sharing a bed tonight.

His boyfriend sat down on the said bed. Preston looked over at Harry.

"I can order us a sleepaway bed if you don't want to share a bed, Harry. I just kind of thought that it would be fun to share a few beds throughout this trip."

This was his last chance to get out of this. At least in his mind, it was. "Um... I mean. I don't... I guess it is fine."

Preston got up and walked over to the phone.

"I know you. I don't want you to be uncomfortable." He started to pick it up when Harry ran over and stopped him.

"Are you sure, Harry?" His boyfriend looked him in the eyes.

"We are just going to sleep right?" Harry asked.

"If that is all you want to do, then that is all we have to do," Preston explained. The curly-haired boy nodded. He decided to take off his shoes and socks and lay on the bed. Preston decided that he wanted to take a shower... alone.

Harry didn't think much of it until Preston walked out and was wearing nothing but a towel. He sat down at the edge of the bed closest to the door.

"Are you going to get dressed?" Harry asked.

"I mean, yeah. In a minute. I was just thinking of something," Preston explained.

"What was that?" Harry asked him.

He shimmied his way next to Preston. Laying his head right next to his lap without actually touching him.

Clearly, this was an awkward thing on Preston's mind because it was taking him longer to say anything.

"It really doesn't matter in the long run. I mean, you and I care about one another, and sex isn't even that important. I was just wondering, though... on the off chance we ever do decide to have sex, would you want to, well you know... Um..."

It was unusual for Preston to be the one stammering. Harry had a feeling that he knew what Preston was asking but didn't want to answer until he said it out loud himself.

"Would you want to be the top or the bottom?"

This was not something that he ever actually thought about when he fantasized about being with his boyfriend sexually.

Harry sat up in the bed, "I don't know to be honest. Well, I mean... I just assumed that you would want to be the top."

Preston looked at him a bit off-put by this answer. "Really? You thought I'd want to be the top?"

Harry had never really put much thought into it. "I mean, would you want me to top you?"

"I know you've only been with one person," which meant Langley. Preston knew that Harry didn't consider his first sexual encounter with a boy to count as sex.

"Did you enjoy it?"

When he had been with his friend Langley, it had not been something planned at all. He had just been outed very publicly and against his will completely.

Harry was having a nervous breakdown after running away. Langley had found him and was trying to comfort him. She couldn't figure out what to do to calm him down. Langley was not the type of person to talk things out. She was all about sex and sexuality. She based her life around it. She did the only thing that she could think to do in that sort of situation, and that was through having sex. The actual sex lasted a second, but everything else took a while.

It had been pleasurable, but that was the last thing on his mind in that situation.

"I can't imagine that being with a girl is the same as being with a guy," Harry stated.

Preston nodded, "I don't know if I have ever told you this, Harry, but I've been with girls before. When I was away at boarding school."

It definitely shocked him to hear this.

"That's cool. Are you bisexual then?"

It had never really come up as to what Preston identified as. At least he never thought it did. At the end of the day, all Harry cared about was that Preston was attracted to him because Harry was very attracted to Preston.

His boyfriend sighed, "I don't think so... I mean, I think sex and love are two different things. Can I get pleasure and enjoy sex with a woman? Sure. Do I really find women sexually attractive? Not really. At the same time, I suppose I could love a woman if it were personality-based alone. It's very complicated. I guess I'm like ninety-nine percent gay and one percent straight."

"For me, I've always just been gay. I don't think I've

ever thought about girls. It always used to be one more burden for me," Harry told him.

The two of them often had serious conversations but usually in the sense of keeping Harry from going and having a mental breakdown. This was one of their most serious conversations outside of that. He looked the taller boy in the eyes and went to kiss him.

"What was that for?" he asked.

"It just felt right," Harry explained.

PRESTON – JUNE 2019

It was nice to have a serious conversation with Harry that didn't automatically send him into a mental breakdown, which Preston knew how to handle at this point. It was just nice to talk with his boyfriend about boyfriend-related things that were on a deeper level.

He knew it was weird to ask Harry if he would prefer bottoming or topping in sex. It just was something that he had never really put much thought into himself. That said, Preston often imagined Harry being the top.

There was just something that really turned him on about the idea of Harry being inside of him and the two of them looking into one another's eyes as they made love to one another. In part, he had to admit that it had to do with the fact that sometimes he didn't like what was in-between his legs. Other times he did. Preston had always been conflicted with his anatomy.

"Do you think you would want to try topping me? You know, when we are actually ready to have sex, that is," Preston asked him; it was nerve-wracking.

This made his boyfriend turn pale. "I mean... I don't know. I'm not like the biggest," Harry sort of said sheepishly.

"I don't care about your size. I'm not that big either," he explained.

It was then that he realized that he was still wearing the towel. "Can I see you naked, Preston?" Harry blurted out very quietly.

"Can I see you naked too?" Preston asked.

Shockingly Harry stood up and took his shirt off. There was no hesitation. He did stop, though, at this.

"I just want to see what you look like unclothed. This doesn't mean I want to have sex. I don't think at least."

Preston nodded in agreement. "Totally understand one hundred and ten percent."

This seemed to be ok with his boyfriend because he proceeded to take off his pants. Harry was skinny but a tad bit toned. His body had always turned Preston on. It was then that Harry took a deep breath and pulled down his briefs. He was standing in the hotel room naked. Preston admired every inch of the curly-haired boy's body. He tried hard not to stare at Harry's most obviously hard member, but obviously, it was what he wanted to see most of all. Harry was cut.

"Harry, you said you weren't that big."

Of course, this made him blush. "I don't think I am," he shook his head.

"So, can I see you now?" Harry asked.

Fair was fair. He got to see his boyfriend naked. So, now it was time for him to show off. Preston stood up and dropped the towel. Harry said nothing. Instead, he moved his hand closer to Preston's crotch. Preston quickly grabbed his hand.

"I don't feel comfortable being touched there right now," Preston exclaimed, which was not the right thing to say. Only it was. Just not that wording and not to Harry, who was sure to get all freaked out. Preston sighed and sat on the bed. Harry sat next to him.

"Please don't think I don't want you. It's just..."

"Are you not attracted to me?" Harry asked more nervously than anxiously.

His athletic boyfriend turned to him and took his hand again. "I think you are the most beautiful guy in the universe."

"It's just you aren't well... you know... hard," Harry pointed out.

"It doesn't mean I'm not horny. I don't know... I have to be honest with you. There are times I don't necessarily like the body I'm in," Preston point-blank told him.

This seemed to throw off Harry. "Why? You have an amazing body."

It was always nice when Harry would complement him on his body. It was the typical thing that someone in a relationship would speak about. He would hope that Harry would still be that way if Preston were not in good shape. However, it was time that Preston set the record straight.

"There are times when I don't like every aspect of my body. Harry, I'm on the trans spectrum."

The curly-haired Knight boy said nothing for a good few minutes.

"Really?" Was all Harry finally said. He looked his boyfriend in the eyes. "Why didn't you tell me?"

"It's not something I've publicly come out about. My family knows but no one else. It's one thing to be gay. It's a whole other arena not to feel masculine all the time," Preston explained.

"All the time? As in there are times you do feel masculine?" his boyfriend asked.

He nodded. "Yes. I'm sure most people do. Just like I'm sure there are times when you feel feminine over masculine. Those can be toxic words, though. I guess the best way to describe it is sometimes I feel confident in my male body, and other times I feel very female and don't like the parts that I've been assigned both from a physical and mental state of mind."

Yet again, it took a few minutes for the blue-eyed boy to respond.

"I mean Preston, I like you a lot. I really do. Like a lot, a lot. There are words I'm avoiding because I don't want to seem too rushed, but I think you know where I am going."

He did, and it made his heart both melt and explode at the same time. "I don't care what you identify as. You accept me for all my craziness. Why would I not accept you?"

This was all he had wanted to hear from Harry.

"Thank you," he said. He hugged Harry and then looked at him. "I just realized we are still naked. I should probably get dressed for bed."

Harry sort of shuffled around. "We don't have to wear clothes to bed. No one is going to walk in."

"I'd like that." This was a positive sign.

It was also a huge step for them as a couple, although he had a feeling there was a lot more to discuss than just that on the surface, which Preston was prepared for, at least in theory. In execution, he knew this was going to be difficult with Harry. The fact that Harry just implied very heavily that he loved him, though, made him think positively.

The two boys eagerly got under the blankets of the bed. "Why is it every cheap hotel feels so uncomfortable and yet comfortable at the same time?" Harry asked in a joking way.

"I suppose that is one way to describe hotels. I don't know. It's been a while since I've been in one," Preston pointed out. He got close to Harry, "I'm shocked our parents were ok with this trip."

The curly-haired boy shrugged a bit. "I think it has to do with the fact that they don't expect us to do anything stupid because I'm here."

Preston would honestly forget Harry's insecurities. They would come and go so quickly. Preston remembered a time before Brad and Langley left where he didn't realize just how bad things could get.

PRESTON -- NOVEMBER 2018

"**S**o, I thought that we could all go to that cute little bistro out in Rochester Hills. They prepare their food so much like this chef that we had back in Manhattan," Langley Kingsley explained to the group.

Her boyfriend, Brad, seemed to have little interest in this. If Preston was honest, he had no interested either. Langley was definitely a character that he had quickly learned to just roll with. She knew how to handle Harry better than even Brad did.

Harry smiled at this. Harry's smile could make the entire room stop and stare. At least Preston thought so.

"I think we should go! It would be a fun double date."

Saying the term double date around Brad was never a smart idea. Brad still did not trust Preston and wasn't fond of always hanging around him. The issue was that Preston made Harry happy, and regardless of whether Preston wanted to be her friend or not, Langley seemed to take a liking to him as well.

It was almost as if Langley's opinion was all that mattered in situations like this. It didn't matter if what she was saying made no sense. It was always going to be Langley's way or no way, which Preston had to admit was fine with him. It was practically the only way to get things accomplished.

Preston himself was not allowed to suggest things to Brad because, heaven forbid, Harry never knew how to make up his mind. Langley was that chaotic neutral that didn't give a damn what everyone else wanted to do. It was her way or no way. In the end, it always worked out rather well. At least the Italian boy didn't mind.

"I'm down for whatever," Preston explained.

Langley tossed her long blonde hair in the wind. "That settles it then. We are going to the bistro!"

This, for whatever reason, sent Brad into a huff and a puff. "You realize we are just getting out of school. So, we are going to drive all the way out to Rochester Hills for an early dinner and then drive all the way back and have school the next day?"

The blonde girl rolled her eyes. "It's called living a little Brad! We've exhausted all the nice restaurants in town. I don't feel like going to the Yacht Club and do not even mention the Harbor Inn. I don't want a cheap burger and fries." The way she stated this as if it was an order, impressed Preston.

"What do you have against the Harbor Inn? It's cheap but good food," Brad said as he crossed his arms, almost offended by this statement. His mother and uncle were constant regulars at the Harbor Inn, which was reason enough why both Langley and Preston did not want to go. They were not fans of running into Vivica. At least not at this time. She was not a fan of either of them. Brad and Harry, especially Brad, did not seem to grasp that his mother did not particularly like the Mobster son nor the Manhattan queen.

"We are going to the bistro." She looked Brad in the eyes.

"If you do not want to come, that is fine. That's more time for me to spend with my favorite couple," as she placed her arms around both Preston and Harry's shoulders.

Brad and Langley were really not meant to be. Harry thought otherwise, but the writing was always on the wall. All they ever did was argue. There was always an issue about something. Sometimes it would be very awkward to witness.

Harry had mentioned, and Langley confirmed in a different conversation that Brad refused to sleep with her. This is where half their issues came from. Preston just didn't understand the attraction that the two had for one another. Brad wanted a Stepford Wife. Langley wanted a sex doll. They weren't mature enough to have this conversation with one another.

"Why can't we ever do what I want?" Brad demanded.

Langley broke free from the two of them and turned around. She looked her then-boyfriend straight in the eye. "Ok, Brad, we will do what you want to do." She turned to Harry, "Is that alright with you, Harry?"

Everyone was looking at Harry now. He would learn later that Harry had texted Langley about the idea of them going to dinner there after school. Harry had trouble formulating ideas sometimes, so he would go through Langley.

Brad was not letting up in this situation. It was clearly pissing off Langley, and it honestly was starting to piss off Preston that Brad couldn't handle being spontaneous for once in his damn life. It wasn't Preston's place, though, to say anything. At least he knew his place within this conversation even though he had no issue with going, and it was very obvious that Harry himself wanted to go.

"I mean, we don't... I sort of... It's just, um..." Harry started to breathe heavily. Brad tried to walk over and comfort him, but Langley stopped him. She knew that it would be up to Preston to calm down his boyfriend.

"Hey, Harry. It's ok. If you want to go, we can go just the two of us. Brad and Langley can go to the Harbor Inn. Or we can wait until this weekend when it will work with your cousins' schedule."

Preston shot Brad a dirty look, which of course, did not sit well with the Fitzpatrick boy, but at the end of the day, Brad could afford to live a little.

Harry held on to Preston. He looked around to make sure that no one was looking and kissed him on the cheek.

"Why don't we go and take a walk," Preston explained as he wiped a tear from Harry's face...

MARY – JUNE 1968

There were certain places the nun honestly wasn't fond of. North Pointe was most certainly one of them. She found the house depressing for many reasons. The gray marble floors, the yellow walls, and the furniture was all white and brown. The natural lighting setups from the windows did not do it any good, and, there was a gawdy mansion across the street that covered the sun.

The nun sat in the drawing-room, waiting for Delia to come downstairs. It was not abnormal for families to invite nuns and the priest over nightly meals. Technically all of the nuns of the Saint Agnes convent were invited to dinner at the Knight house. They all knew that they would be treated to a very good meal, but they also knew the Knight family's reputation; not in the sense of Benton's extra-marital affairs, that was rather typical. It was the fact that Benton was a prick, Delia was a known drunk, and the son that didn't run away was a little shit, for lack of a better word. It was honestly a nice way to describe Rodrick.

Rodrick happened to be sitting across from her in the

circular room. He was reading a sports magazine. It was probably something much more salacious, but he was hiding it well.

He looked up and over at the nun. "So, do you just enjoy stocking my family? What do the nuns all gather when you return, and do you tell them about how dysfunctional we all are?" the teenage brat asked the blonde nun.

Mary raised an eyebrow at this. "Not only have I been your teacher, but I've been your mother's friend for a number of years. Do you think that low of me?" Mary asked in response.

She could understand this from the perspective of the town at large. When she did go over to other families' homes, they would gossip about the rest of the town because they thought it would earn them brownie points with the Church. The Church members didn't understand that the priest and none of the nuns honestly cared about how sinful their next-door neighbors were or that they themselves were rather sinful. Their money and free meals were still welcome. The town was full of dysfunctional people.

"I don't judge your mother for you and your father's actions," Mary said as she leaned her head on her hand.

Rodrick now raised an eyebrow at this.

"Aren't you supposed to not judge any of us?" he wondered out loud.

"So, you turn eighteen soon, right?" Mary pivoted away from the conversation.

The drawing room doors opened, and Delia walked in with Benton. They were both dressed relatively well, considering that it was just her.

"Mary!" Delia said.

The nun rose from her seat and gave her friend a hug. She casually waved at Benton.

The married couple sat down across from one another in armchairs. The four of them all sat in silence for a moment.

"I'm just going to cut the ice," Benton said as he crossed his legs, "We saw each other at Saint Agnes the other night. I trust that aside from my wife and your frumpy redhaired friend, you haven't told anyone," Benton stated.

He definitely stated it. He most definitely didn't ask. "I really have no comment on that," Mary explained.

Obviously, she hadn't told anyone else. She wondered if she would have told the police had these people been strangers to her.

"I just don't want you telling people things out of context, any more than you already have," Benton told her.

Mary refrained from rolling her eyes. It was obvious that the car mogul was attempting to threaten her. She wanted him to. She really did.

"So then... I was invited to dinner. Are we going to eat?" Mary asked.

PRESTON – JUNE 2019

It was as if time had drifted, but Preston had remained awake. It was close to three A.M. Harry had drifted off to sleep. The Italian boy thought about it for a moment and realized this was the first time that he had ever seen his boyfriend sleep, and there was something about seeing the curly-haired Knight boy with his eyes closed so calm that comforted Preston.

Were they meant to be together for the long run, or were they meant to be a memory along the way? Preston had no idea. He hoped if, for whatever reason, it was the latter that they would at least end on good terms. He never had any intention of breaking up with Harry, though. Through all the Knight boy's faults, he had to admit at least to himself that he loved the man with the curly hair and grey-blue eyes.

HARRY – JUNE 2019

Last night was thrilling. He had often thought of what seeing Preston naked would be like, and it was better than his wildest dreams. He wasn't sure how he felt about the fact that Preston didn't know what gender he was, or maybe he did. It confused Harry. There were so many things about modern gender politics that he just didn't understand. It wasn't that he didn't respect the concept of them. It was that he hadn't paid much attention to them in the past.

Referring to someone as they or them sounded like a plural form. Gena was the only person he knew that referred to themselves in this way. Yet, they also still identified as a female. He supposed that he could have asked them to explain it further, but Harry always got nervous that he would offend someone. That was never his intention. In his mind, it was better to stay ignorant in silence as long as he let those around him live their life. The difference now was that his boyfriend might have been one of these people. Well, not might; it was evident that he was.

The two continued to drive. Harry took his headphones

off, "You know I could have driven even if just a few miles out."

"I'm aware. I told you, Mr. Knight, no driving until we are on our way back," Preston said without turning away from the road.

The blue-eyed boy sighed, "I have a question."

"If it is about where we are going, forget about it," Preston told him.

"No... I was just wondering about what pronouns I'm supposed to use around you now that I know," Harry explained.

Preston scratched his head. "I um... I guess he and him still. I don't really mind being called a man. I know that in terms of society, I am. However, at the same time, I just like to be pretty sometimes. At least as of now. It could change."

"Like with the dolls?" Harry pointed out.

"I never really thought about it, but I suppose. I don't know. My parents never really steered me away from dolls as a child. My father would surprise me with them. It wasn't that I didn't play with action figures, which are totally dolls themselves. They are all just miniatures or figurines. I personally call them dolls, though.

The dolls really didn't bother Harry. He would play with Hope and Hannah and their toys when he was younger. It was just a bit bizarre to walk into a teenage boy's room and have a very large shelf of fashion dolls, some of which were in lingerie. "I mean, I'd totally collect them with you if you wanted."

This made his boyfriend laugh, "Collecting anything is a rabbit hole that is easier said than done. You start with one and end up with a hundred or so."

The last thing Harry needed was an entire room dedicated to one thing. The thought freaked him out. He was reminded of his aunt's *closet,* which was actually a guest room transformed into a giant closet from all the clothes she had acquired over the years. She had outfits that she used to wear at the Hutchens fashion shows still wrapped up, never worn more than once or twice.

His father's comics were in the attic along with pretty much his entire childhood that he seemed to latch onto for some reason, even though it seemed like Cliff Knight had the most traumatic childhood out of anyone that he knew.

"Do any of your friends know about the dolls?"

It was weird to ask him this, but Preston did have friends who were not technically friends with Harry from sports, clubs, and stuff.

The Italian boy shrugged, "One or two very close ones that I've known forever. They don't really mind. I really don't bring people over to the house, though. It isn't like I'm going to bring a two-hundred-dollar doll to the park or something."

Harry wasn't sure if he liked Preston's friends or not. He remembered when Preston first started to appear in his orbit as a child. It was such a different world back then for the two boys.

HARRY – JUNE 2015

It was summertime. His mother was gone for a few months, so Cliff arranged for Vivica to spend an afternoon with Harry. Brad was home for the summer from boarding school. They were twelve or thirteen at the time, but age was irrelevant to people in Grosse Pointe. They arranged to go to a park. Aunt Vivica and his sister Hannah caught up together while the two boys played.

Brad wanted things to be like when they were younger before puberty started to hit. Harry didn't know how to be that version of himself anymore. He no longer had the drive to like sports nor pretend to like sports. It was also around this time that he had been the loneliest. The people around him were so distant now and not as they had once been.

"Ok, you hide behind the tree, and then I will go make a sneak attack on you!" Brad whispered.

Harry had absolutely no idea what he just said, but he did what he was told and went and hid behind the tree. He stood up straight and tall and waited. He didn't know what he was waiting for or what game exactly they were playing. That was when the tanned Italian boy with striking brown eyes ran towards him with a group of boys.

Preston was still friends with all of them to this day. He had seen Preston in school before, but it was only upon seeing him here in gym shorts with a tight t-shirt that he sort of really noticed him. He had a smart-alecky mentality that often freaked him out in class.

Brad stormed up behind Harry and gave him a dirty look.

"I don't like them. Let's go somewhere else," he said, grabbing his hand.

Preston noticed them and walked over.

"Hey, do you guys want to come over to my house? My mom just got me a new waterslide!"

Would they be shirtless? Harry had no idea why that was the first thing he thought about when a waterslide was mentioned. He just knew that a part of him really wanted to see Preston and his friends without their shirts on.

Brad got in front of Harry. "We are going to a water park. Besides, we both have pools at our houses."

"Why are you freaking out, bro?" Preston asked Brad. He seemed a bit thrown off at how rude Brad was being. Harry was thrown off as well.

"Just because our dads are friends doesn't mean we are," Brad explained. He crossed his arms.

The rival boy looked at Harry.

"Well, what about you? Do you want to come over, Harry? You don't have to do everything that your asshole cousin does."

Brad shoved him. It was then that aunt Vivica ran over.

"Bradly Fitzpatrick! We are going home now. You do not shove people, especially not the son of Jackie Carson-Costa. That woman is nuts. The last thing I need is her saying that I provoked you into doing that. Christ, your father wants to have dinner with Anthony and that whack job later in the week. I swear I will make you spend the week with your aunt Margot if Jackie starts squawking her mouth again."

HARRY – JUNE 2019

Preston had wanted to spend time with him back then. This made Harry smile.

"Do you remember the time you invited Brad and I over to go swimming when we were younger?"

"You mean the time that Brad shoved me, and your aunt trash talked my mom?" Preston asked. He kind of gave him a weird look at this.

"In all fairness, your mom trash talks my aunt all the time. But yes, that time. Did you ask us because you wanted to spend time with me even back then?" Harry asked.

This made the Costa boy smile. "Yeah. I admit that I had a little bit of a crush on you back then. It wasn't until the end of last summer that I really started to think about you in the way I do now, though. I mean, we were so young at that time. You always had the cutest eyes, though."

"I wish you had asked me to hang out more often. Especially when Brad was away at school," Harry lamented.

To think that he and Preston could have been friends earlier on.

Preston sighed, "Mr. Knight, I tried to hang out with you constantly! You never wanted to." He took his eyes off the road for a second to inform him of this.

He had wanted to hang out before. This was news to Harry. At least he thought it was.

"When did you want to hang out?"

The boyfriend once again sighed, "Oh, Mr. Knight... I'd try to get you to be my partner in things all the time. Or I'd make my friends offer to invite you into my group. Don't you remember me picking you in my groups when we were in gym class together?"

It was strange, but Harry was just now putting all this together.

"You've really liked me for that long?"

"If I weren't the one driving right now, I'd be bashing my head against the steering wheel. Yes, Harry Heathcliff Knight. I have had some form of a crush on you in one way or another since probably kindergarten. There I said it out loud. I've liked Harry Knight since forever!" he started laughing hysterically.

This was always lost on Harry. He felt bad in a way. "I was just always lost in my head. If I had known... I mean, it took me until like fourteen to realize that I clearly liked guys and then probably another year to accept that I was clearly gay."

"And that's when I went away to boarding school myself, of course. I had wanted you to be my first kiss so bad, not going to lie," Preston admitted out loud.

"Well, you kind of were my first kiss that I accepted," Harry explained.

Preston decided that they needed to take a little break from the road and pulled over at a rest stop. They were somewhere in Indiana at this point. He parked the car.

"I'm just going to ask, what was it like to be in the situation that you were in?"

It took Harry a moment to process what he meant. He realized what situation he was referring to. Todd Roberts...

"It's something that happened. I was being stupid."

Harry felt Preston put his hand on his shoulder.

"You were not being stupid. You were put into a really fucked up situation."

It had officially been a year since the court case and the settlements. Todd was supposedly in a juvenile detention center. He remembered the day that Todd was sentenced. He was screaming at the top of his lungs that Harry enjoyed what they were doing. He claimed he was only getting arrested because Harry's family had money. Things like that made him wonder.

"Todd had just been nice to me in the moment. He was attractive, I guess. Admittedly he wasn't really my type. However, he was a guy showing me interest." That's basically the gist of how things started.

"I wish I had been around. I would have made that boy pay. Even though we really didn't know each other, I would have made him pay for his actions," Preston explained.

Things like what Preston just said were what would frighten Harry. Did Preston have that sort of power through his family? What exactly would have happened?

"Did you see the video?" Harry asked?

"I mean, yeah, I saw it. One of the guys from Saint Agnes sent it to me while I was in Italy. It wasn't very easy to watch, given the context of what was happening. I can't believe people could find that funny or even get off to that. It was you being taken advantage of."

That was the sad thing. That video was filmed earlier in his experimentation with Todd Roberts. After a month or so, Harry didn't really want to hang out with him anymore. He didn't like that all they ever did was sexual things. He wanted to hang out. Harry thought that Todd had wanted to be friends or more than friends, but all he really wanted was oral sex from him. Obviously, Todd wanted more because he would say as much, but Harry really wasn't ready. Luckily, he was never forced into doing more than just oral sex.

However, the way that Todd would go about it was hard to get over, especially once he revealed that he had recorded it.

"He'd call me a rich little slut. He'd say that I just wanted to piss off my parents. I wasn't gay. I just wanted to make my wealthy family mad. I was just like my aunt. A whore in the making. He'd force me to get it all into my mouth even if I couldn't breathe. Then when I couldn't, he would hit me."

He didn't realize it until now, but Preston was crying. Harry reached across the passenger seat and gave him a hug.

"I'm alrig- I'm better than I was. It's in large part because of you. You treat me like a human being. I love you, Preston Costa." He didn't care if it was too soon or not anymore. He needed Preston to know that he was in love with him.

Preston wiped his tears as he held Harry in his arms, "I love you too."

Harry looked up very glassy eyed at him, "Really? You aren't just saying it because I said it?"

"Oh, Harry... Oh, Harry... I think loving you has become the most natural thing in the world to me," he said as he smiled at Harry. It only made the Knight boy's heart melt more. He ducked down a bit and kissed him on the lips. Harry loved his kisses. Every single one of them was a magical gift.

SUSAN – JUNE 1968

"I don't really have an issue with the Costa family if I'm being honest," Brandon told his sister.

Susan understood where he was coming from. They were nice to them. At least on the surface. It wasn't like they were outwardly being criminals. Susan was just taking what Mary had said to heart a little bit more than she should have.

Susan shook her head. "I just want us to be careful," Susan told her younger brother.

Brandon shrugged. "So, how will you get out of this date when it inevitably happens?" Brandon asked the older sibling.

Susan shrugged herself now, "I'll just humor it probably. Not out of fear for the Costa's but because mom and dad will have a manic episode as per usual."

She knew how her parents acted when one of them went against something that could be for the benefit, supposedly of the entire family.

"I mean, you shouldn't have to keep playing the charade for the two of them," Brandon whispered.

Susan's heart skipped a beat. "I'm not really sure what you mean by that," Susan rambled. She went back to cleaning up the bar.

Brandon looked around the room. Aside from a few people playing pool and Mrs. Templeton passed out at her regular spot, nobody was there.

"Susan, you are my sister. I've seen you look at Mary the way I look at Nadia," Brandon explained.

Susan looked at him, and her eyes widened. She didn't even say anything and ran into the kitchen. She started to breathe heavily and needed this feeling to stop. Did she make it that obvious? Did her parents know too? What about Mary and Delia? Was it that obvious?

Brandon walked in and stood in front of her.

"Please don't be mad at me. If you aren't that, then I'm an idiot for even suggesting it. If you are, though, then I don't care. Until Nadia, it's always been you and I against the world. You know that," Brandon explained to her.

Susan was still breathing heavily. She closed her eyes, "I am that way, but mom and dad… and the Knight family… I can't let people know about these things."

Her brother put his hand on her shoulder.

"Look, maybe you can't be yourself here, but there are places you can go. Nadia is insistent that once we graduate that we see the world. So, if you went to one of those places, I'm sure we would visit regularly. San Fransisco, New York City… I don't know. Idiot Rodrick's older brother ran off to Holland to be more accepted with his now-wife. Obviously, there are places you can be you," Brandon told her with a smile.

"Yeah, well, what about our parents? They expect me to run the bar, which is a main source of income right now, and then get married, apparently to a future mob boss."

Susan sat down on a stool. This was all too much at once for her.

"Look, our parents have been chasing a pipe dream since we were toddlers, if not before that. Our father isn't going to live long enough to see where things go with the fortune that he is insistent that we will one day have. I want Nadia. I don't want that money. You seem completely indifferent. When the day comes, and I really don't want it to be any time soon, I guess I'll settle down in that house they are building and run the company. But you should be able to live your life now," the curly-haired boy explained.

She knew he was right. It wasn't even their parents that had kept her around. It was Mary. It was Delia. Yet, she had no future with Mary in the way she wanted, and she knew it.

"Maybe you are right."

Susan just wasn't sure how she would present this to her parents or her friends.

PRESTON – JUNE 2019

They decided to stretch their legs a bit. They would be out of Indiana rather soon. Preston knew that as soon as they were in Illinois, he would have to tell Harry that they would be going to Chicago, which he hoped that he would take well. It was what he planned for them to do in Chicago that had him a bit worried.

The conversation that they just had was honestly the deepest the two boys had ever discussed with one another. Preston had wanted to ask him about Todd Roberts for the longest time but never wanted to make Harry feel pressured.

They would discuss the trauma on the rare occasion because Harry would have his episodes where he would remember something and not be able to get it out of his head. The curly-haired boy would never say what he was thinking about, though. It made Preston almost want to vomit, thinking of how sick it really was.

He remembered the link that had been sent to him. It was on a porn website labeled as *Slutty Rich Boy likes it*. It wasn't a sex tape. It was blackmail. It was torcher porn. It was rape. It was disgusting and horrendous. A part of him wanted to call his father or Uncle Jack and have them send someone to the juvenile detention center this Todd was at and have him pay for what he did to sweet and innocent Harry. However, Preston wouldn't do that.

Preston had to learn not to be his father. He wouldn't allow himself to be a mob boss or even a mobster, for that matter. The family business was not a business that he had any desire to get himself involved in. He wasn't better than his father for not wanting that lifestyle. He just learned from being around his parents that there were better ways to use the power they had against the world. You did not have to use guns or violence to be a powerful person.

When he was younger, there were times when he had considered being a lawyer or getting into politics. His uncle Jack had to explain to him rather early on that he could be whatever he wanted but that the world would not necessarily treat him the same way that they would treat others in the same role. He would be revered but not always for the right reasons.

It was always Uncle Jack that would have to be the voice of reason for his dysfunctional family. Preston was ready to escape the world of the mob. He knew it would never truly happen, but it would be easier with college and the rest of his life because he would be separated from his father and his business. He just knew that it would be difficult for Harry to understand this concept and potentially run from Grosse Pointe. It just felt like it would make the most sense for them to be able to run together.

Today was a giant turning point in their relationship. He knew that there was still a lot left to uncover with Harry's traumas, but that was fine. They would as time went on. There was no need to rush things when they didn't need to be rushed. However, it felt great to hear Harry say that he loved him. It had been difficult not to scream it from the rooftops himself over the past few months. It wasn't too soon in the slightest. It was the perfect time. He actually meant something to the man that he loved more than anything in the world. Harry meant something to him too. Harry Knight loved him. Harry Knight loved Preston Costa. He just wanted to keep repeating that over and over in his head.

"Ok. Are we ready to get back on the road?" Harry asked as he walked back over.

Preston practically jumped onto him and started to hold him in the middle of the rest stop where people were around. He started to kiss Harry.

"Preston, we are in public."

"I don't care!" as he continued to hang on to his boyfriend. "I'm in love with Harry Knight!" he said very happily.

As he said this, a woman with a "*Can, I speak with the manager*" haircut walked past them and very casually but loudly said, "Fags. Burn in hell!"

He could sense that Harry was starting to tense up. The Sicilian in Preston started to flare up, and he marched over to the lady.

"You want to say that to my face?"

The woman got right in his face, "You two are little fagots. Fagots will burn in hell."

She tried to start walking, but Preston put his hand on her shoulder and prevented her.

"Let go of me. Who do you think you are?"

"The son of Anthony Costa. You might not know the name, but you will feel differently when your ass looks him up in a little bit. I see you drive a Knight car. Funny, do you know who my boyfriend is? The heir to the Knight family fortune."

He gave her the finger and walked away. That was not the best way to handle things. Again, the goal was to escape his family's image. At the exact same time, though, it was nice to be able to lean on the fear that the family name could bring.

He walked back over to Harry, "Sorry about that lady. She is a worthless piece of shit. Don't let what she said get to you."

Unfortunately, it was too late, and Harry was having trouble breathing. Preston quickly started to hold Harry.

The Costa boy managed to get them into the backseat of the car. Preston held on to Harry for dear life as he took very deep breaths in and out.

"Breathe, Mr. Knight. In and out. Just keep going in and out. No one matters but you and me. I'm here to protect you always."

He put his head to Harry's. He loved to do this. It just made him feel close to the boy.

"Why... why... why are peo- people so mean? I just want to live my life. Why Preston?" Harry sobbed to him."

He wished that he could take all of Harry's fears and

trauma away from him. If the boy could he would, for Harry.

It was easier said than done. The world had been so cruel to Harry, and sometimes Preston needed to be reminded of that for the context of their own relationship. The fact that he could possibly worry about such stupid things when Harry dealt with loss, abandonment, neglect, and abuse...

"Remember what we just told each other? We love each other. You and I love one another. That's what is important, Harry. Not some random bitch probably breaking every commandment in the Bible and going against whatever else it says in there. Straight, white, cis people use that book as a way to remain guilt-free with their own issues. Their favorite line is mentioned less than anything else, and that freak probably cheats, lies, and steals on the daily."

This got a chuckle out of Harry. "There is that beautiful Harry Knight laugh that you know I love hearing."

His boyfriend wiped his own tears. Preston took his hand and did it himself. "How do you put up with me?"

Preston kissed him on the cheek, "Very easily." He looked at Harry, who now had a slight smile. "Your kisses make my heart melt." Harry buried his face into the back of the car's seat. "That's what I always think when you kiss me."

"It's as if we are one another's destiny," the Italian explained. There were so many forces that could have kept the two boys apart, and Preston honestly refused to let that be the case. He could remember very well when he told his parents that he was going to ask Harry to the Fall dance.

PRESTON – OCTOBER 2018

"You said you had something to tell us?" Anthony Costa asked his son.

Preston sat in the living room with his parents. He sat on an office chair while his two parents sat together looking concerned and intrigued on the love seat. He cleared his throat.

"Yeah... so, um I have something to tell you guys."

His mother nodded. "Well? What is it?"

He decided to the best way to go about this was by making it sound like great news. Which it totally was. "I'm asking someone out to the Fall dance."

His father smiled. "That's wonderful. Let me guess you need money for a new outfit or something?" He quickly took out his wallet. However, Anthony's wife put her hand on his to gesture that he not so quickly whips out the wallet.

"Is it a boy or a girl you have asked?" Jackie asked. "It's a boy." Preston explained. His parents were of course supportive of him experimenting with his gender and sexuality. They just weren't always sure of what he would say or do in terms of it. "He's honestly a pretty great guy."

Jackie nodded. "Well, who is this boy? Who is his family?"

"See, this is why I felt the need to sit you guys down..." Preston explained.

"Oh, dear lord you're going out with an older man." Jackie rubbed her forehead. Why was this what his mother would jump to? "What? I don't have daddy issues!" Preston blurted out.

His father took a deep breath. "Well, I'm glad to hear that." His father turned to his mother. "Jackie I'm sure the boy is perfectly fine."

Preston was now the one rubbing his forehead. "It's Harry Knight."

"Oh shit... Not Cliff Knight's son." Anthony said. He sort of looked at him as if he should run.

His mother sat in her seat for a moment. She then stood

up and started to walk back and forth. "Harry Knight... The son of Tiffany Knight. The nephew of Vivica Weston-Fitzpatrick-Knight-Fitzpatrick-Fitzpatrick. Harry Knight. I don't think that we can approve this relationship."

His father looked at Jackie. "I don't think we are both coming from the same place with this, Jackie. If he wants to be with the Knight boy let him."

"Think about what you just said. The Knight boy. Our son with the Knight boy." Jackie explained.

It was weird to hear his parents refer to Harry as *The Knight Boy, a*s if he was that kid who was a known shoplifter or sacrificed a squirrel in third grade, and the entire town witnessed it. Yet, when Mrs. Templeton baptized the town's squirrels, it was considered normal. Why on earth did Preston think about Mrs. Templeton? That old pile of bones with a thin layer of skin on top. He was going to throw up just thinking about her.

"Look, guys, I like Harry Knight. He's really sweet."

Preston started to blush a little. He never blushed in front of his parents. Anthony looked at Jackie like it was a losing battle for her. She sighed, "Ok, I will support you going to the dance with him. I just think that you need to be careful around that family. The only decent Knight or

Fitzpatrick is Nial."

Her husband rolled his eyes, "It wouldn't kill you to get along with one woman."

"I get along with Annabelle," Jackie crossed her arms. Preston wondered if and when Annabelle was ever going to come back from boarding school.

"So, then we are all in agreement that I am taking Harry Knight to the dance?" Preston asked his parents.

"If you really feel the need, then sure go for it. No one is going to stop you," Jackie explained. She looked at Anthony. "Now, you take out the wallet," she said as she rolled her eyes, got up, and stormed off.

Preston got up from his chair. "I think that went well," as he looked to his father for reassurance.

"You are going to want to keep that boy close. I can't promise your mother won't send a hitman after him," Anthony joked. The sad thing is that it was something his mother would do.

PRESTON – JUNE 2019

Harry started to wipe away his tears. "I think I'm ready to get going again."

Preston played with Harry's curly hair a little bit. He could tell his boyfriend loved it when he played with his hair.

"We can always just sit here if you want." Preston told his boyfriend. Harry shook his head, "No. I'm ready."

HARRY – JUNE 2019

Why did I have to react to that? Why do I always do this to myself? Harry, you need to learn to fight your own battles. It isn't fair that every time you freak out, Preston or Hannah or dad or aunt Vivica have to be your defender. Preston will not stick around forever if you can't figure out how to handle such simple tasks as interacting with people. Oh, for crying out loud! Stop thinking about this, Harry!

Supposedly they were getting closer to wherever it was they were going. Harry made a promise to himself that they could spend a week watching baseball games, and he would keep his mouth shut. He was not about to ruin Preston's week any more than he already had, which made him suddenly realize maybe that could be exactly what it was.

Were they about to spend a week watching baseball games? Could there be a place where there was a weeks' worth of baseball even to watch? Harry was now dreading the thought of having to watch a week's worth of baseball. A week of not being able to figure out who was winning the game. A week of it being hot.

Brad used to take him to Tiger's games all the time when they were younger, during the summer when he would be home. Harry loved getting to spend time with Brad. He hated everything else about the experience. This would be no different.

"Ok, we just made it into Illinois. Surprise... we are spending a week in Chicago!" Preston said. He turned to his boyfriend to see a reaction.

Harry put on a brave face, "I can't wait to watch baseball!" Did he just blurt that out loud? He definitely did because Preston was looking at him very confused.

"Um, well, we aren't going to any baseball games. I mean, we could, when we get back to Detroit, I guess. I didn't know you liked baseball."

Harry didn't. He remembered a conversation between him and Langley when it was still football season. She essentially told him that you don't go to the games to watch them. You go to support the guy you like, as in, the guy that you want to screw while he wears the uniform, but Langley loved sex. Langley loved sex a little too much looking back. Harry still missed Langley.

"Sorry, I was in my head. No, we don't need to go to a baseball game. Chicago. It's been a few years since I have been in Chicago."

Ok, this could actually be a fun week. Normally, when he was in Chicago, his father was on business, and he ended up stuck in the hotel room for the bulk of the trips. Preston started laughing, "To be in your head, Mr. Knight - that's the dream now, isn't it?" He smiled at Harry. "So, then we are going to do the typical tourist stuff. We are also going to do some more gay stuff, I guess would be the most politically correct thing to say."

Gay things? He thought they had already discussed the topic of sex, and apparently Preston wanted to leave the state in order to do it?

"Well, I have no idea what you mean."

His boyfriend laughed, "I had a feeling you wouldn't. We are going to go to a few clubs. We are going to see some drags. Then we also have tickets to a drag pageant. The Miss Queer America pageant, to be exact."

There was both a very straightforwardness about how Preston said this but also a giant hesitation.

It wasn't that Harry had an issue with the concept of

cross-dressing. It was just different. It wasn't something he understood.

Then Harry realized that Preston didn't necessarily identify as a man. Instead, Preston had a love of dolls and wanted to explore the world of makeup.

"Do you have a desire to be a drag queen Preston?" He asked.

The Italian kept his eyes on the road. "I don't know, maybe. Is that a problem?"

"I mean, I've never really been around a lot of cross-dressers," Harry admitted. If any at all, he guessed.

"Ok, first things first. They aren't cross-dressers. They are performers who are creating art that goes beyond gender norms," Preston told him.

Again, he had no issue with the concept of this. He just knew that a lot of these drag queens could be mean. He thought of the time that Langley showed him this queen online that used to say the meanest things ever.

"Are they going to be mean to me? I can't handle people being mean to me right now."

"Harry, we are going to a pageant in an auditorium. We will be sitting at a table watching as these performers compete. They will be too busy trying to win the crown to notice you. I'm sorry to inform you of that," Preston seemed a bit annoyed with that response.

"Well, what kind of gay clubs are we going to be going to?" Harry asked. "Preston, we don't have ID's! You are still seventeen!" he reminded him.

Damn it, Harry! I just told myself that regardless of what Preston wants to do, we will do it. At least it isn't baseball. Lord, I hope I didn't plant the seeds for him to think that I want to go to a baseball game. I really don't want to go to a baseball game.

"I mean, I guess we will figure our way around it," which he tried to say as calmly as he could.

Preston nodded, "Don't worry, Mr. Knight. I have everything under control. My mom knows some people who own some clubs out here."

He mentioned this as if it was normal to know other gay people. Outside of the GSA and Preston, he really didn't know any gay people. He sort of assumed that Langley was pansexual, considering she had sex stories with just about every person on the planet.

Langley.... he still missed Langley. Harry looked down at his phone. The Knight boy knew that it was pointless to text her because she wasn't going to text back. That said, he wondered what she was up to. He imagined what it would have been like to have gone on this vacation with her and Brad. Harry knew that Brad would have been just as bad if not worse on this vacation, though. It would have been him and Langley arguing nonstop the entire time.

"I think we are in Oakdale right now."

"I've never heard of it," Harry admitted.

"It's supposed to be a nice little town. We will go through Bay City as well. Springfield is out of our reach, though. We should be in Chicago in two hours or less," Preston said.

Two hours and they would finally be in Chicago.

"I'm going to take a nap then. Wake me up when we get there." Harry gave Preston a quick peck on the cheek.

"This isn't fair, Mr. Knight. I have to keep my eyes on the road while your beautiful self is sound asleep. It's going to be very difficult to keep my eyes on the road."

Everything about Preston was simply perfect. He

always knew exactly what to say. Harry gave him one more kiss. He then reached into his bag, took out a Xanax, and slipped it into his mouth before closing his eyes. He wanted to be as calm as possible once they reached Chicago.

***

Harry opened his eyes, and he was no longer in the car. "Preston?" he called out. Where was his boyfriend, the curly-haired boy wondered? It appeared he was back in Grosse Pointe. He was sitting on a bench outside on Langley's front lawn.

"Hey, Harry!" she said with a smile on her face.

"Langley! What are you doing here?" he asked her.

The blonde girl smiled and looked straightforward. "You know that you need to give me up, right?"

This confused him and hurt him a bit.

"What do you mean?" Harry asked.

She looked at him and took his hands, "Oh, Harry, we had a wonderful year together. You truly were the best friend that I ever had. It's time to move on, though. You have Preston. That Gena girl is a bit frumpy for my taste, but they seem nice. You can't live in the past forever."

Off in the distance, Harry could see Mrs. Templeton streaking while Holly threw singles at her.

"This is a dream, isn't it? This isn't really happening." It meant that he didn't have to give up on Langley.

"It might be a dream. It might be the wake-up call you need. Pun totally intended. You know I love a good pun," she explained to him.

"You definitely aren't the real Langley. If you were the real Langley, you would be shooting f-bombs left and right," he explained.

The imaginary Kingsley girl sighed, "Unfortunately, the F word has to be used sparingly. You aren't in Grosse Pointe right now after all."

This conversation was very disjointed and just made Harry feel sad. "I'm sorry, but I don't like this conversation anymore. I just want to wake up."

She started to drift into space again. This was Langley, but it wasn't Langley. Langley would be sighing and grunting far more than this figment of his imagination. It was like a distorted memory.

"So, you are going to Chicago? It's fun for a weekend getaway, I suppose. You know me, though, Manhattan through and through, except during the summer when we go to the Hamptons. I'm probably at the summer home right now. That's one of the properties my father was able to get back."

If this dream wasn't going to end, then he needed to just stop talking to the fake Langley.

HARRY – SEPTEMBER 2017

"**H**arry! Get down here," screamed a familiar voice. It was one he had not heard in some time. The curly hair boy realized very quickly that he was still dreaming, only this time it felt more like reliving a memory than it did talking to a fake version of someone. The Knight boy walked down the grand staircase that led to the North Pointe foyer.

"How long does it take to get downstairs, Harry?"

It was his mother, Tiffany. She was wearing a red turtleneck with black dress pants and a pair of stilettoes. She had a pair of pearls on that had once belonged to his great-grandmother.

"I'm sorry. I just overslept again."

His mother rolled her eyes, "It's your first day of tenth grade, Harry. Do you really want me to be embarrassed?"

"I don't need you to drive me," Harry explained.

He knew why she was driving him, though. A few weeks earlier, they had run into a group of women out shopping, who had sons around his age at Saint Agnes. They made a comment on how she was never around. It stuck with his mother, and she made it a point to drive Harry to his first day of school.

She kept talking about joining the PTA that year. There wasn't a PTA at Saint Agnes, though. There was a parents committee. It had the same basic idea, but you had to eat, sleep, and breathe school spirit. It was basically something that the women whose husbands managed to find them a house within the Grosse Pointe community joined to show status. Tiffany was a bit late to the game, and on top of that, she had no time with her busy schedule at the hospital.

"Can I have breakfast first?" asked Harry. This was the wrong thing to say. "If you had been down here a half-hour ago, maybe. We need to go so I can walk you in." Why on earth was she even trying right now?

"I'm um... Ok." He really had forgotten how much his mother wasn't much of a mother. She was so obsessed with being Tiffany Knight.

There was a knock at the door. Harry went to answer it, but Tiffany held him back.

"We have staff. It's their job to get the door."

It took literally two minutes. Harry remembered this very clearly. Two minutes and more knocking before a person on their staff finally ran to get the door.

None of the staff ever said it out loud, but when Tiffany and Cliff finally divorced, he could tell that they were just as happy as his aunt had been, which was who happened to be at the door.

"I need to speak with Cliff."

"Why on earth are you here right now?" Tiffany scoffed. She put her purse around her shoulder and started to walk towards the front door and around Vivica.

"Come on, Harry. We are going to be late!" They weren't, though. They were actually going to be way too early.

His aunt could tell that he wasn't happy. "Isn't today your first day of school?"

"Oh... um... yeah. It um. It is," Harry told her.

She smiled, "I remember my first day of tenth grade at Saint Agnes. Your father and I nearly didn't make it ourselves. Brianna Belle, our childhood best friend, was ready to kill us for being so late. I really wanted to have breakfast before school at the Harbor Inn. Well, back then or well, I'm sure it is the same now, the diner was so packed in the morning. I was insistent, though, that I get some eggs and toast."

Tiffany sighed, "Yes, well... that was then, and this is now. Cliff is at work, and regardless, I've told you not to come around unless you call first. Do you really want me telling Nial that you were out looking for Cliff again? Honestly, Vivica, why can't you just stick with your man."

His mother got a text. "Damn it. I'm needed at the hospital." She looked at Harry, "You are going to need to take a car to school or something," as she quickly shuffled towards her car.

He didn't even want her to drive him to school. Why was she such a terrible mother? Why did he think that about his own mother? Was this part of the memory, or was he only thinking this, looking back at the memory? He remembered what happened next, though. His aunt put her hands on his shoulders.

"Well, since your father isn't home and since I don't want to go back into the office, why don't we continue the Knight-Weston family tradition of trying to get me some eggs at the Harbor Inn?" She looked at him and gave him a kiss on the forehead.

"I'd like that," Harry said with a smile. "Just we can't be late."

"You and Brianna Belle would get along so well," Vivica explained.

As they started to walk towards her car, Mrs. Templeton walked out onto her front lawn with a sign that said *Whites Only*.

DELIA – JUNE 1968

This dinner was not going well, and the housewife could tell. Mary was giving more dirty looks to Benton than usual. Rodrick was just rambling nonsense, which wasn't unusual, although he usually knew not to bring that to the dinner table. Yet somehow the breakfast table was perfectly acceptable.

The doorbell rang.

"Who on earth would ring us at this hour? Anyone with sensibility knows that you don't show up at someone's house during their dinner hour," Benton barked.

One of their maids walked in.

"Mr. Knight... um... Mr. Costa is here to speak with you," she explained and then exited.

Benton jumped up from his seat and practically ran into the foyer.

Delia looked directly at Mary. They were sitting next to

one another.

"I didn't know it was Luca Costa he was dealing with directly!" she shrieked.

The nun shrugged her shoulders.

"It wasn't the other night. It was one of the goons or henchmen or whatever you call them," Mary explained.

"Hitman," Rodrick spat out.

The two women looked at him now.

"What? That's what they call a person like him," he told them and then went back to eating.

"I'm sure it is nothing to worry about," Mary told her.

That wasn't what she was saying the other day, though. So, clearly, she thought otherwise.

Delia didn't want to deal with this. The Knight family was just toxic. They couldn't go six months without some ordeal.

"I'm going to ask him to leave," Delia explained. She looked at both Mary and her son, "Yes... I'm sober."

The family matriarch marched herself into the foyer, where Benton was discussing something with Luca.

Luca looked up at her and smiled, "If it isn't Mrs. Knight. Looking spectacular as ever."

She wasn't sure who he was trying to flatter or why he was even bothering. Italians were too much for her. It probably had something to do with her Hispanic blood, along with the similarities and differences.

"We were having dinner," Delia explained.

"I know exactly where you are going with this. Sadly, I cannot stay with Mrs. Knight. I have to get to a little pow-wow in Detroit this evening. We could probably set something up for later in the week."

He stopped for a minute and was clearly thinking about something. She had no idea what he could possibly be thinking about, but it frightened her.

"Actually, why don't you all come to my house this Sunday for dinner. The Fitzpatrick family will already be joining me. Your friend, the nun who I see in there...," he said loudly so that Mary was sure to hear him, "Is more than welcome to join us as well. In fact, I practically insist upon it," Luca said.

He waved goodbye to Delia and shook Benton's hand. He then exited himself.

Delia walked right up next to Benton.

"Well, this is just great," she told him.

"I know; we have to have dinner with the Fitzpatricks," Benton sighed.

The wife turned to her husband. "That's the negative side you found to this ordeal? The fact that you have to have dinner with the Fitzpatrick family again?" she screamed at him.

"Once in a decade was more than enough," he said in a serious tone. He looked at his watch, "I need to go make a phone call."

He walked up the grand staircase. He wanted privacy because they had telephone lines in basically every room in the house.

The nun walked over to her. "How on earth did I just get invited to dinner at Luca Costa's house?" she demanded. "Again, I'm sober," Delia said as she rubbed her forehead.

Rodrick walked out of the dining room. "Oh, good lord,

does this mean I have to be in the same room as Brandon Fitzpatrick? That towny gives me such a headache," he shook his head.

It concerned her that both her husband and son were more concerned that their dinner guests consisted of the blue-collar Fitzpatrick family and not the fact that the host for the evening would be a known kingpin.

HARRY – JUNE 2019

"Mr. Knight... Oh, Mr. Knight. Time to wake up!" the familiar voice of his boyfriend said.

Harry tossed and turned a bit, reawakening. He started to open his eyes. They were in a parking lot of a hotel somewhere in Chicago. He noticed the name. It was a Fitzpatrick hotel. Brad's Aunt Margot had just ventured into the hotel market with Langley's sister Lucy in charge of overseeing the entire process. Lucy wasn't going to be here, though. He knew that. She was off in California, opening a hotel there.

"Ok, this is a step-up from the place we stayed the other night."

"I thought it would make you feel closer to home," he smiled, which was essentially the dressed-up version of saying that his parents got him a good deal because of their friendship with Nial Fitzpatrick.

The two boys got out of the car. Harry stretched his

arms and legs. He was wearing a yellow polo that was not tucked in, and his shirt was riding up on him. Preston was totally checking him out, and this, of course, made Harry get turned on. He hoped that they spent as much time as they could outside of the hotel room. It was clear that sex was the last thing either of them was looking for this weekend, but at the same time, it was clear they were both open to changing that.

The air smelled differently in Chicago. It wasn't a bad smell. It just was different. Harry was used to living near the unofficial sixth Great Lake and smelling the air that went through those waters. He was used to the silence of Grosse Pointe, which was odd because Grosse Pointe was far from a silent place to live. It just was on the manicured lawns where the town had an unspoken agreement to keep their battles to the confines of their living rooms and foyers. Only on occasion would you see or hear someone going nuts outside, aside from Mrs. Templeton. The town just turned a blind eye to her bigotry.

They made their way into the hotel. He was sort of disappointed. It was nicer than the place they had stayed the other day, but even so, it clearly wasn't that much nicer. It was just a typical hotel. The main difference was that it had a restaurant, a bar, a luxury hair salon, a spa, and a boutique, all in the same building.

This hotel clerk seemed to be a bit more into their job, but with that came an attitude that Harry was not very fond of.

People were lounging and doing other things. Lots of people talking on their phones or scrolling through them. As they made their way into the elevator, it felt all too familiar.

"We have dinner reservations tonight at this place that is supposed to have the best Chicago-style pizza."

Harry was about to point out that neither of them liked Chicago style.

"I double-checked. They have other things on the menu." Clearly, Preston had thought of everything.

It took a few minutes for them to make their way up to the floor they were staying on. It was towards the top. They walked down the hall, and the room was labeled *Suite 1001*.

"We are staying in a suite?" Harry was a bit shocked.

"Nothing but the best for Mr. Knight," Preston winked as he used the keycard.

He turned the doorknob, and they walked into a

charming living area with a view of the city. Harry immediately walked over with Preston. "Wow, you can see the entire city!" Preston said with excitement. He looked at Harry. The two looked at one another, and Preston leaned in to kiss him.

MARY – JUNE 1968

"So, we are all going to be there?" Susan asked, a bit confused as she walked down the path outside Saint Agnes.

Mary nodded. She wasn't really sure how things had escalated like this.

"Delia claimed she was sober, but there was just a little too much courage in her voice when she went to talk with Luca," Mary explained.

The two stopped and sat down on a bench. Mary could tell there was something else going on with Susan beyond the regular.

"It will be fine. I mean, I'm sure it will. The Costa's are Catholics, so I doubt they intend on killing all of us if I am there; you would assume at least."

This didn't seem to get the reaction she was hoping for from Susan.

"What's wrong, Susan?" Mary finally asked.

Her strawberry blonde friend finally turned and looked at her. "I think I might want to move out west," the Fitzpatrick admitted to her friend.

This definitely shocked Mary.

"Why would you want to move out west?"

Susan took a deep breath. "I think that my story here is over. At least for now. I guess I don't know what else to say," Susan admitted to her friend.

This threw Mary off with a mix of emotions. Susan had become one of the best friends she had ever had.

"What will you do out there?" Mary asked.

"I have some savings, and I've already found a women's run hotel that I can stay at for a month or so. I have management experience with running the bar. At the very least, I can find a serving position," Susan told her.

It was very obvious that Susan had put serious thought into this, which made it even more shocking.

"I just can't imagine a world without Susan Fitzpatrick

in it," Mary admitted.

There was something different about Susan from most people in her life. She was so quiet and peaceful most of the time. They had a lot in common in that way.

"I don't know if I can handle this, but I want you to be happy."

Mary tried to smile, but it was hard given the circumstances.

"I suppose you can look at it from this angle; we'll always be together at the bottom of our hearts. We just won't always be physically together," Susan tried to offer up as a consolation.

It was a nice sentiment, but still.

"When are you leaving?" Mary asked.

"Well, I still have to tell my parents and Delia. However, I have a one-way ticket for Tuesday," the strawberry blonde told her.

SUSAN – JUNE 1968

"**I** forbid it! Your mother forbids it! You will not move to California!" Seamus screamed at his daughter in their living room.

Susan wanted to cry. She knew this would be hard on her parents but didn't realize that it would make him start yelling. Her mother kneeled next to her and held her hands.

"Susan, my child. You have to stay. You are a single woman without a husband," her mother redundantly told her.

She looked over at Brandon, sitting with Nadia in the love seat across from her. Brandon looked scared.

Nadia, however, stood up. "Mrs. Fitzpatrick, this is probably the best thing for Susan. Imagine what it would be like for her to explore a man out west. They have all that west coast money after all." Nadia was looking at Seamus as she said this. "I bet you there must be someone with gold still out there. Imagine it now!" she held her hands out. "Susan gets married to a man in the gold business, and then Fitzpatrick Steel becomes Fitzpatrick Steel and Gold!" Nadia claimed.

Brandon now sat up. "I don't think that is the case out there anymore," he said as he looked at her.

Nadia turned and gave him a sour look. As bizarre of a suggestion as that was, she appreciated that Nadia was trying.

Susan looked at both her parents, "I'm sorry you aren't happy about this, but my life is practically non-existent here."

She stood up.

Ida stood up with her.

"You will find a husband, and he will work with your father. Or he will have his own money already."

Susan took a doubletake at her. She was being serious. She knew that her mother supported her father's antics, but she didn't think that she had the same mindset for real.

"You can't possibly think I want to marry for money and not happiness." She looked at her parents again, and they were not answering. "You two didn't marry for money."

Susan looked to her brother to say something.

Nadia once again stepped forward. "I mean… marriage should be about love. Although I find the concept of marriage a bit difficult to handle," she shrugged.

Brandon quickly looked at her, and so did her parents.

"You don't believe in marriage?" Brandon asked, a bit shocked in tone.

"I didn't say I didn't believe in it. I just think that the concept can be difficult to handle. Who wants to go through with that kind of thing?"

Nadia laughed at this.

All but Susan were looking at her directly.

Brandon definitely looked hurt.

She told her brother constantly that he needed to be

more open with Nadia about his feelings. They clearly were in different places.

Susan moved towards the hallway.

"I'm sorry, but I will be moving to San Francisco," Susan said.

That was final. She stormed down the hall and into her bedroom, although it wasn't her childhood room. They rented a home a few years back as they started building the mansion. Yet all of her childhood things remained. She sat down on her bed and looked up at the ceiling. As she did this, she could hear someone slam a door shut. It was probably one of her parents. There was a knock on her door now.

"Come in," she said as she assumed it was Brandon and or Nadia.

"Your father is going for a walk," Ida explained. She sat down next to her on the bed. "I just wanted life to be easy for both my children. I remember the day you were born. I had promised always to make your life easier than my own."

Ida's face sunk a bit. Susan could tell she felt a bit of guilt for how their life had turned out.

I mean, look at how things went. I had two loving parents and a kid brother that I love."

Susan smiled at her.

Ida shed a tear. "Yes, but you aren't like the rest of us," her mother explained.

Susan's heart skipped a beat. "I don't know what you mean," Susan whispered.

"Yes, you do. I've known since you were a little girl. I just thought that maybe you would grow out of it," Ida shrugged.

Susan really didn't know how to process it.

"That's not really how it works," Susan admitted.

"Well, I know that now. I guess I still hoped that you would maybe want to live the life your father and I mapped out for you."

While she knew her mother meant well by this. It was not exactly coming off as very kind, in her opinion.

"I should be able to live the life that I want. I know it isn't going to be easy. But for me, to marry a man would be too difficult. Yes, there is a part of me that wants children. I'd be a good mother. But I can't live in misery with a man to accomplish that. Even if that man was incredible on paper," the daughter told her mother.

Ida nodded, "I understand. Just promise me

you will be safe and write regularly." She hugged her daughter tightly.

"Ma, we have things called phones now," Susan laughed.

Ida looked at her daughter, "Do you really think your father will be ok with long-distance calls one way or the other?"

She gasped. Susan supposed she had a point.

PRESTON – JUNE 2019

His uncle Jack had been insistent that this restaurant was a Chicago staple. He had the utmost confidence in anything that Uncle Jack told him. Preston now realized, though, that the best Chicago anything was a loose cannon of a statement. It was like picking which Coney Island had the better hot dog, American or Lafayette? If you asked someone from Grosse Pointe, they would automatically say the Harbor Inn, which had a good dog, but it was too easy a choice.

Why on earth was he thinking about hot dogs in a pizza joint when he had Harry Knight, the most beautiful guy in the world, sitting across from him? He could be eating cardboard, and it would still be a perfect evening.

"Ok, you said that there would be more than just pizza on this menu," Harry reminded him. He had this little smirk on his face that was driving him wild.

Preston looked over the menu himself. "They have wings and burgers," the Italian boy pointed out.

The Knight boy sighed, "I know they do, but you know very well that pizza joints that do burgers and wings usually don't sell a lot of them."

"Ok, so then we get pizza," Preston sighed. This week was going to go down perfectly if he had to fight for it, which, knowing Harry, he would totally be fighting for.

"Ok. We are asking for no sauce and extra cheese."

This was definitely something that Preston should have thought about a bit more. At the end of the day, this was a week about opening up the world that Preston wanted to live. A life where he could be more in tune with himself but with Harry around him. If this worked out, he intended for them to come back to Chicago every few months. Sure, they could entertain the concept of New York City because of Langley, but his parents would never allow it.

There was a reason the Costa family lived in Michigan. His father, Anthony, made too many mistakes in the NYC mob. The target on Preston's back would be no more. They would just paint him red and tell him it was open season.

The Costa boy nodded, "That sounds fine, to be honest. I mean, it's pretty much cheese bread, but it is fine."

Really it was. He had to admit he preferred New York-style over Chicago. He preferred New York-style over Detroit style as well.

"I'm excited to check out some of the clubs tomorrow."

This was where Harry was supposed to nod in agreement. "I'm just hoping they aren't too loud," Harry said.

That was a better response than he honestly hoped for or expected from Harry.

"I'm just excited to spend time with you," Harry added.

That was what Preston needed to hear.

"Great because that's what this week is about. Non-stop togetherness."

The moment he said that out loud, he wondered if that was actually a good thing or not.

"So, where are the drag queens? Let's bring on the drag queens!" Harry said as if he was reading from a script.

It was sort of obvious that Harry was trying his hardest to be comfortable in a situation he had no idea how to react to, which he both admired and was a bit annoyed by if he was honest with himself. It wasn't that difficult to try new things, but for Harry, it was always a problem. He knew that there was a brave face happening right now.

"We are just at a regular pizza place. I don't think that many drag queens go out in drags just to eat pizza."

"What are drags?" Harry asked very innocently.

Valid question but self-explanatory, Preston thought. "It's just slang for someone in drag."

For whatever reason, Harry pondered at this for a moment, "See, I'm willing to learn!"

"Oh boy, Harry. What do I do with you sometimes?" Preston said very lovingly, even if there was a tone of annoyance that he wished he could have given off.

SUSAN – JUNE 1968

"I forbid this!" Delia screamed as she sat out by the yacht club pool.

Susan had a feeling that this would be the hardest conversation.

"Nope, not going to happen. If you don't like living at home, you can live in the pool house at North Pointe. We don't use it for anything."

Susan started to laugh. She knew they didn't use that house for anything because it was disgustingly dirty.

"I just need a change in my life. You've become one of my best friends along with Mary over the past few years. I don't want to say goodbye, but I need to live my life to the fullest."

Delia rubbed her forehead, "Then get married to one of Benton's business partners and hire a pretty maid to be your lover. It's a tale as old as time."

She needed a drink badly.

"You know?" Susan asked. She wasn't as shocked for some reason.

"Of course, I know you're gay. You were hiding it?" Delia asked bluntly.

The strawberry blonde wasn't sure how to respond to this.

"I mean, I assumed Mary didn't know, so I never said anything out loud. But come on, you and I have a special bond; you're in love with Mary. I'm your best friend. You might be Mary's best friend, but you know what I mean." Delia rubbed her forehead again.

Sadly, Susan did know exactly what she meant, and Delia was correct.

"I guess best friends do know those sorts of things. Why did you never confront me?" Susan asked.

Delia took a sip of her iced tea. "You never brought it up, and it wasn't my place to. After you got married, I just assumed you would discuss an affair, and we'd just bond over that."

Delia shrugged.

"Are you having an affair, Delia?" Susan asked.

This made the Latina woman laugh, "I wish. Oh lord, Benton is terrible in bed. But that's because the bastard is having affairs of his own. He doesn't have time for me, and honestly, I don't have time for him if I am being honest. Or well, I don't really want him anymore. But no. No affair on my end."

It was honestly shocking how normal this conversation was between her and Delia. No, it was not normal in the sense of the subject matter. However, Delia never spoke like a normal person, and that is what made this normal.

"Thank you," Susan told her.

Delia shrugged and smiled a little. "I'll just have to come to visit you often. You aren't going to get rid of me, Susan Fitzpatrick. Besides, Benton's sister keeps threatening to move back home. Sarah Knight is a bitch. The less I see of her, the better. Lord, I could use a drink right now. I won't have one, but I would love one." Delia winked at her.

PRESTON – JUNE 2019

The evening went on for the two boys. Preston slowly started to realize that Harry hadn't been anxious since they got to Chicago. There was definitely hesitation in his voice, but he wasn't freaking out about anything. They walked down the street together, and Preston took his hand. Harry looked at him and was now looking a bit concerned.

"Relax, Mr. Knight. We are in a big city. Two boys holding hands is far from the craziest thing that these people have seen today."

Harry smiled, "You know my aunt always called my father her Knight in shining armor. I think you are my doting prince."

This made Preston blush. "I mean, that sort of makes you my Knight then. My protector?"

"Well... I think you are more my protector." The curly-haired boy frowned at this.

The Italian boy stopped walking and looked Harry in the eyes, "I think it is safe to say that you and I will always protect one another no matter what."

"Most definitely," Harry said with a very sincere smile. "I do have a question for you if you don't mind me asking."

Harry didn't look him in the eye, "I was just wondering about the guys before me. You've mentioned people in Italy before."

A fair question. One filled with old wounds.

"There were two people primarily. One was actually a girl like I've mentioned. She was nice and attractive, but something was missing. However, I think we both understood that it was just sex. Then there was my roommate."

Sergio Brilli.... they were the same age and height. Sergio had the best lips he had ever seen until Harry, that was.

"Sergio was something I wanted but apparently couldn't have."

"I don't understand what you mean by that," Harry explained.

Preston wasn't sure he even knew what he meant. Sergio screwed with his head pretty badly.

"I think that I caught feelings relatively easily with Sergio. However, Sergio was only looking for release." At least, that is what Sergio had claimed.

The two boys had become relatively close over their first semester. Sergio was the one wearing the rainbow bracelet when they first met. Preston was more reserved about being out. The moment they locked eyes, they were clearly drawn to one another. If anything, Sergio was more drawn than Preston was. It didn't take long for Preston to immediately fall for the native Italian boy.

Preston realized that it was lust at first, but as time went on, the two shared everything with one another. It took Preston a while to realize that Sergio was not open about his life with him. Yes, he would share things like he had siblings and was not close with his parents. However, he realized that Sergio was just not revealing everything when Preston was revealing all his details.

It didn't help that when they were in class or around campus or in town even, he didn't want to be around him. It was only in their dorm room. At the end of the semester, Preston discovered that Sergio had requested a room transfer. He claimed that he wanted to be closer to his soccer or football friends, whatever the hell they called it over there. Preston was left alone for much of the second semester, thinking that Sergio must have just been experimenting with him. That had to have been the situation. He probably had a girlfriend.

Then, it was revealed that he had been dating a boy across the hall from his new dorm, and he was openly dating him.

"Sergio was a lesson," Preston looked off into nowhere.

DELIA – JUNE 1968

After having lunch with Susan, she needed to get her mind off things. The Knight matriarch went shopping at the Hutchins shopping center in Detroit and probably bought at least one of everything on the floor she was on. Benton would probably scream at her eventually, but he would get over it. He always did.

She walked in through the back door and sat down at the kitchen table. She was hungry but knew that dinner wouldn't start for another hour. Benton probably would be late as usual, but she could hear noise coming from the library in the next room. It was probably just Rodrick on the phone with some friend of his.

Delia had no issue with bursting in on her son because he needed to be reminded who was in charge most of the time. She got up and opened the door to their library. Instead of Rodrick, however, it was Benton. He wasn't supposed to be home. He was with Luca Costa. Why was this man back here?

"Delia. Why are you in here?" Benton demanded of her.

"I just got home. I heard voices. I thought it was Rodrick on the phone or something."

Luca did not look as he did the night before. He was almost villain-like in the facial expression he had right now. Yet he was still smiling.

"Mrs. Knight. How lovely it is to see you again. I trust you are looking forward to our meal tomorrow. I know I am."

He walked up to her and put his hand on her shoulder. Delia did not like this and wanted to leave. She looked at Benton, who was not looking back at her. The coward.

"I'm just having a little conversation with your husband about the importance of being on time with payments." He looked at his watch. "I suppose I will see you both tomorrow," he said as he exited the library.

Delia waited to hear the backdoor shut. "Benton Knight, what did you get us into?" she demanded.

Benton was still not looking at her.

"I told you that I had things under control. You don't need to worry yourself."

He sat down in his father's old armchair. He used to listen to old records while he sat there. Benton was a pale imitation of his father.

Delia was never a big fan of Heathcliff. He wasn't a fan of herself either, but he was still a man, unlike Benton, who was a little boy.

"If you had things under control, then you wouldn't have low-life scum like Luca Costa in our house. The concept of a Costa at North Pointe. Your father would never have allowed it," she spat out.

"Look, our sales were down last year. I needed to find new distributors for certain products. Luca reached out and was very cordial at first," Benton explained.

Delia was baffled, to say the least. "You thought that working with an organized crime boss would be smart? The Costa family is bad news, and you knew that," Delia screamed.

"I did, but my sister has been on my neck lately with phone calls out in California. She wanted results, and she wanted them now. That's why she keeps threatening to come back out here. She is threatening to take my spot as CEO," Benton admitted.

The Latina wife couldn't help but laugh.

"Your masculinity is so fragile that you couldn't handle your sister coming and taking your position?" she screamed at him.

"It's my position! Mine." He jumped up and got in her face, "I'm the one who moved back in after our mother got sick. I'm the one who our father constantly berated," he screamed.

Delia turned around. She couldn't look at him.

"You are also the one who slept with the maid that your father was smitten with," she said softly.

"Oh, get over it. It was a one-time thing, and it was years ago now," he reminded her.

She couldn't just get over it. She was reminded of it every week at church when they ran into Lana Brash and her husband, David Brash, and their little boy DJ. He looked nothing like David, though. He did look a lot like his brothers Rodrick and Clifton. Benton thought she was too stupid to notice. Maybe he was too stupid himself to notice. However, she knew.

"Did you at least pay her off?"

Delia was a lot of things. She was an alcoholic. She was a bad mother herself. She wasn't a monster, though. Delia didn't want the world to know that DJ Brash was really Benton's bastard son because of revenge sex. However, she wanted to make sure that a brother of Clifton and Rodrick would be taken care of.

"You think I'm going to pay for that child? He has a father. He has a name that isn't connected to the Knight name whatsoever."

Benton sat back down in his late father's chair. The smug look on his face. He looked like a child being forced to share his toys.

Delia could hear someone from the next room. She had enough of Benton and went back into the kitchen for one moment. She assumed it was one of the house staff members.

It wasn't. It was Rodrick. She looked at him right in the eyes, "How much did you hear?" she demanded.

"Enough," Rodrick said.

She rarely ever saw her son look vulnerable. She wanted to comfort him. However, she also knew that certain guidelines needed to be followed with the information he now possessed. Lord knows why she stayed with Benton, but she did, and as his wife, it was his duty to protect him.

She went and sat next to him on the back staircase. "You can never tell anyone that you know this information. That includes your father," Delia explained.

Her son looked at her. Rodrick was clearly confused. She could see it in his eyes.

"Mother," he said in a smug tone. "I knew that dad screwed Lana Bloom or Brash or whatever she wants to go by now. I couldn't care less about the piece of scum he is. What I'm upset about is that you were in there trying to take control. Are you trying to ruin our family?" He stood up.

Delia sat there staring into nothingness. This boy was her son. She birthed this little monster.

"I swear, mother, get yourself together. You've been in this world longer than I have," he said as he walked upstairs.

HARRY – JUNE 2019

Their first night had gone over well. It was the second time they had ever shared a bed together. Strangely though, they didn't cuddle through the night. It was as if they were both just too mentally exhausted from the road trip. A lot had been revealed in a short amount of time.

Harry felt a sense of being closer to Preston than he had ever been in the past, which he was grateful for. It was as if both boys had thrown everything on the table, and neither was turning down anything being offered to them.

If the Knight teen were honest with himself, he had to admit that this was really not his idea of a vacation. Then again, he had to admit that he never knew how to act during vacations, so if this is what Preston wanted to do, he will act like it is the best thing ever. It could be for all he knew. He was genuinely excited about where things could lead the rest of the week. Harry still had no idea what a drag pageant was, though.

Preston was still asleep next to Harry. This was the

guy, the person that he could potentially spend the rest of his life with. He needed to take a moment to think about this. They were still so young. Yet, it was a thrill and a rush and not in a way that was going to send him into a panic to think that he and Preston could potentially be together forever.

Stop Harry! You are too young to be thinking about forever. I mean, yeah, Preston is awesome. He accepts you for who you are, a semi-basket case, and that's being generous. He was a full-blown basket base. Preston accepts me even though we both very much know that I'm a mental case. He makes me want to be better. If it weren't for Preston right now, I'd be sitting in my bedroom until my dad and aunt Vivica returned from their trip. Then, I'd be dragged out of the house for awkward family time that no normal teenager has with their parents. If Preston weren't in my life, would I have ever had a real relationship? Oh boy, Harry, we really gotta stop asking these questions to ourselves.

The Costa son started to open his eyes and looked over at the curly-haired Knight boy. "Good morning. Did you sleep well, my Knight?"

"Yes. I slept very well. It was a nice deep sleep." It actually was. There was no fidgeting or weird thoughts as he drifted off to bed. "How did you sleep?"

His boyfriend started to stretch, "I slept great. Are you ready for our first official day of fun?"

Harry did hesitate but then looked Preston in the eyes, "Yes. I am actually ready." The two boys smiled at one another.

"Good. We have a welcome thing at the pageant. Then we are going to do some museum stuff afterward. It kind of starts out a little 'out there' for you but will calm you down afterward. Then we will see where we are at," Preston explained as he got out of bed.

They were both semi-dressed this time, but Preston's bulge was very noticeable when he got out of bed. It took a moment for the Costa boy to realize that Harry had noticed.

"My eyes are up here, Harry."

That line made him think of Langley for a second. "I'm just... I'm excited." He got a little giggle out of Preston, which was kind of sexy coming from his deep voice.

"I don't mean it like that. I mean, I'm excited to spend the day with you outside of our little bubble."

This got a smile out of his boyfriend. "I am too. We are going to have a lot of fun this week. We are going to have a lot of fun this summer in general."

"Oh, yeah, I'm so excited to fill out college applications," Harry said quietly.

"Like you have anything to worry about. You have beyond perfect grades," Preston pointed out.

This was true. "You and I both know that good grades mean nothing anymore. There are tons of people with good grades who will be applying to the schools that I would want to get into. I have no extracurriculars."

He knew he could get into a good school. It just wouldn't probably be the best of the best for this reason. It wasn't as if he intended on going to Harvard, Princeton, or Yale.

However, the University of Pennsylvania or Duke sort of interested him. At the same time, he had no desire to live in the south, even if just for school. Plus, it was located in North Carolina, where those bathroom laws happened. Not that it would apply to him. Yet could it apply to Preston? Was this a question that eventually would need to be asked for his boyfriend? As in, *hey Preston, what bathroom are you going to use going forward?* There was a lot about this gender stuff that Harry was going to have to adjust to.

"We can figure things out together. All I care about is

making sure that we can work out our schedules if we do end up at different schools," Preston explained as he put on a blue sweater. He looked good in blue.

"That's kind of far out to be thinking... I mean, not that I don't want us to be together by then. I hope so much that we are. I mean..." Harry wished he could have a rewind button.

His boyfriend just laughed, "I know what you mean. You don't always have to explain things, Mr. Knight. It's ok to let me choose subtext for myself."

It wasn't that he worried about Preston, not understanding subtext. It was that Harry himself was worried that he wouldn't get the subtext.

***

This pageant thing was being held at an auditorium somewhere downtown. It was a so-so venue compared to the theatres he had been dragged to by his family over the years. Harry had to go to many events held at the Detroit Opera house, the Fisher, Fox, etc., which were all very nice venues.

There was some out-of-state stuff that was also pretty cool if that was what you were into. Harry wasn't, but then again, he had no idea why he was putting so much thought into this. The two boys were placed at a table in a section for a brunch-type situation.

Harry had heard of drag brunches, but he had never gone. It seemed like they were amongst a mostly older crowd. They weren't there specifically to watch any certain performer. Apparently, there was a Michigan queen that would be there, but Harry knew nothing about them. Their drag name was Lydia Bug, which sort of felt anti-climactic if he were honest. Not that he knew much about drag names but still.

If Harry was honest, he was a bit nervous about being around all these queer people. He knew that he had no reason to be, but it was definitely different.

Preston took his hand, "Are you ok?" his boyfriend asked.

The Knight boy smiled, "Yeah. I'm legit good. Just, you know, it's different."

"Yeah, but different can be good," Preston smiled.

As they continued to look at one another in the eye, two men sat down at their table.

"Hi!" said one of them. He was in head-to-toe pink, but all of it was designer. They both appeared to be in their late thirties or early forties. "Oh, don't you two look so cute. You must be new here."

"We are!" Preston explained. "This is my boyfriend Harry Knight, and I'm Preston Woods." Woods was Preston's fake last name that he would use when meeting strangers. The Costa name, even out of town, still held some baggage to it.

The man in pink turned to the guy he was with, "Oh, how charming! Well, I'm Lloyd Powers, and this is Christof St. Germain."

The only way one of these men could come off as being more flamboyant was if one of their last names was Cummings. Harry was both set back at how over the top they were but also was holding back giggles. He knew that would not be appropriate, though.

"So, then am I correct? Is this your first time at the pageant?" Lloyd asked.

Harry slowly nodded, "Yes. I mean, yeah, it is. We are on vacation, and yeah." Of course, he just answered the question three times.

"You are just adorable!" Christof said. He was very animated in his body language. They both were.

Preston took Harry's hand, "Are you two a couple?"

Lloyd started laughing. "Oh God, no! We left the hubbies back in Philly. This is a little girl's week out. We go to all the major pageants. My husband prefers to be stuck in his office all day long," as he rolled his eyes. "Are you two in college?"

"High school. We are from Michigan ourselves," Preston explained.

The two older men smiled at one another. Harry chose to take this as innocent.

"Starting young?" Lloyd stated.

"Hardly Lloyd. Drag is for everyone nowadays. At least that's what the internet says," Christof explained sort of sarcastically.

Harry was not sure if he liked these men individually or together. They just seemed a little too over the top for his comfort zone, and yet Preston was eating up every second.

"I've never been to a drag show before."

His boyfriend put his hand on Harry's arm and rubbed it. "It's going to be fun. I promise!"

"I'm going to check out the buffet," Lloyd explained.

"Anyone care to join me?"

He was clearly looking at Preston, which sort of threw Harry off. Preston nodded and got up along with him.

"Great! We will be back. You girls talk amongst yourselves."

It always made Harry cringe when someone would refer to him as a girl, even in a positive sense. It might have been different for Preston.

He looked at Christof. "So... you guys come here all the time then?"

Christof smiled, "Oh, since we were just a little older than the two of you. Not on such of a grand scale. We are children of the Atlanta Ball scene. We moved up to Philly later on."

This was something that Harry only knew a tiny bit about. Preston had made him watch *Paris is Burning*. It wasn't a bad movie. It just freaked him out as all old movies did.

"So, then you two are drag queens yourself?" asked Harry.

"Well, Lloyd still dresses up. I've sort of given it up. My husband and I travel a lot, and you have to pass for straight people, of course," Christof frowned.

Pass? He had heard about that before. It reminded him of something to do with the GSA.

"Is it hard to pass for you?"

"As time has gone by, life has gotten easier. People are more open to things, which is both a blessing and a curse," the older gentlemen explained.

It was hard for Harry to put his finger on it, but there was something off about Christof. A sort of sorrow that seemed always to be there. It was something that he felt he could relate to in some way.

"How is it a blessing and a curse? You would assume that being able to be yourself would be a good thing."

The older gentleman brushed his hair out of his face, "Oh, trust me, it is."

Harry noticed that he used his hands a lot to articulate.

"It's just...well, as wonderful as it is to see two younger men at one of these things you probably discovered drags through TV and online culture. Which, don't get me wrong, is absolutely wonderful. It's just that things like drags and ballroom used to be for us. It is something that you and your boyfriend would discover in your own time, as opposed to people who have gentrified it."

Gentrification? Could something like cross-dressing... drag... or whatever it was actually be gentrified?

"Can a way of expression be gentrified?

"Yes and no. It's hard to explain. You probably never had to deal with being ostracized by the people around you," Christof explained.

Harry was about to point out that his mother and sister had not been close with him. However, then he realized that he still had his father, aunt, another sister, cousin, Preston, his family; and several others like his aunt's maid Holly and Langley's brother and sister that still lived in town. He was not kicked out of his house when he was outed.

The bulk of Harry's family supported him. They wanted

him around. His mother had since reached out to him, and while they would never be close, she didn't exactly seem to hate him. "No... I guess I don't."

PRESTON – JUNE 2019

"So, now you and the quiet boy... you make a cute little couple," Lloyd said as they waited in line for the buffet.

It always made Preston feel proud when someone complimented them.

"Thanks. It's been like nine months. He's actually nervous about being here right now."

Lloyd smiled, "Oh, he has nothing to worry about. Well, just some petty gay men, but you are bound to find that anywhere."

He seemed to be joking about this, at least somewhat.

Preston hoped that the rest of the week would be like this. Lloyd would definitely be a good guide throughout the pageant. He just had a feeling.

Lloyd himself noticed a few people and waved.

"Preston, if you don't mind taking my plate back to the table. I need to go and catch up with a few people," Lloyd explained.

Preston nodded in agreement.

The Costa teen looked over at his boyfriend and smiled. Harry was handling this situation better than he thought he would. Obviously, he was trying to be supportive, which Preston both appreciated and was annoyed with at the same time. Harry needed to be Harry, unfiltered and scared of the world around him. That was the boy he liked so much. The boy that he really loved. He walked over to Harry and sat back down.

"So, what are you guys talking about?" Preston asked with genuine curiosity.

Christof looked directly at Preston, "I was just telling your boyfriend about the generational divide between your generation and our own."

Christof took a sip of a drink. "You know, as in how LGBT people are looked upon and how LGBT people view things amongst themselves," Christof further explained.

Oh great, Harry was probably playing ping pong in his head over this.

"Well, I mean, I think Harry and I are just really discovering queer culture ourselves in many ways. This whole trip is a part of that," Preston explained.

Christof stood up. "I hope you kids get what you are looking for in the experience. I need to use the little girl's room. I'll be back."

Lloyd was definitely the optimist in that friendship.

Preston looked over at Harry, "Are you ok?" He knew he wasn't. "The truth Mister Knight," the straight-haired boy smiled.

Harry sighed, "It was just a lot to digest all at once, I guess. I mean, we are a lot luckier than a lot of people. At the same time, though, I just look at how my mom treated me when I was outed. The way those strangers treated me when that video of me was released," Harry explained.

Preston understood where Harry was coming from.

"I think that learning to acknowledge our privilege will be a difficult situation, but I think together we will be able to humble one another in learning how to cope with it," Preston tried to say as eloquently as possible.

The one thing Preston loved about Harry was that he

could be naive about the world around him. However, he could be frustrating as hell to deal with at the same time. The world was not black and white. The world was filled with a billion shades of color, and Harry could sometimes have trouble seeing that.

"So, are you excited about our senior year?" Preston asked in curiosity.

Harry sighed at this. "Yes. It will be fun to be a senior, especially because you know..." Harry grimaced.

Preston didn't know but was intrigued. "No. I don't know, Mister Knight. What do you mean?" he asked in intrigue.

Harry got bashful, which was, of course, adorable.

"You know... I have a boyfriend going into it, which will be cool," Harry smiled at this.

The mobster's son couldn't help but start to smile himself. "We do make one another blush a lot, don't we?" Preston joked.

"I suppose we do," Harry said.

***

Christof and Lloyd gave them their number to hang out later on. Harry got the wrong idea of what that meant, and of course, Preston had to spend an hour explaining to him that it wasn't what he thought. Preston had other plans in store for them that evening.

"How are we going to get into a gay bar?" Harry demanded to know.

The Costa boy smiled. They weren't going to drink. They were just going to enjoy the experience. He had wanted to go to one of the ones back home in Detroit but knew Harry would freak out because, at the time, neither was over eighteen. However, Harry was 18 now and could enter legally. It was Preston, who was shy of being eighteen. It wasn't like he didn't have a fake ID, though.

"Let's just focus on having fun tonight," Preston said as they walked out of the lobby and onto the sidewalk of the Fitzpatrick hotel where they were staying.

Harry was nodding uncontrollably.

"Harry, they will think your real ID is fake if you act like that."

He tried his hardest not to roll his eyes at this.

"I can't help it, Preston! I just don't want us to get in trouble. What if you get arrested?" his boyfriend asked.

Both his parents and uncle had been arrested on many occasions. None of them had ever had the charges stick, though. It would be the same for him.

"So, then we will only be here for a little bit, right?" Harry asked.

Why on earth was he asking this?

"I mean, we will have to see how the evening plays out. There are other gay bars and clubs in this city Harry." Preston explained to him, trying not to get frustrated.

The Costa boy knew that Harry was not a fan of large group settings, but this would be an experience; their first gay bar together.

They walked past a crowd, and a few queens were standing outside. One happened to have a wig on that looked almost like cat ears. It was rather charming. She was telling a story that Preston could hear the end of... *"This is just like when I had my Heathers the musical-themed birthday party at Applebee's where I invited my ex!"* they said with excitement.

Harry overheard this very clearly and was giving them a look.

Preston grabbed him by the arm and brought him to the club, where of course, there was a line. He brought some bribe money just in case they didn't get in naturally. He honestly had no idea if that was a thing people actually did or not in real life.

"This is going to be fun. Aside from school dances and the People of the year Gala's, we have never really danced together, just to dance," Preston said as he held onto both of Harry's hands while they waited in line. This made the Knight boy smile.

"I'm not against us dancing. Loud music, though, Preston," Harry explained.

Preston understood where he was coming from. He honestly just wished there was a way to make Harry less anxious.

The line was slow, but they eventually made it to the front. This was going to be the real test for Preston. Harry gave his ID and, of course, was shaking. Out of both of their IDs though, his was actually real. The bouncer let him in.

Harry stood to wait for Preston. He held out his ID with confidence. It was not a cheap fake ID. The bouncer looked at it for a second longer than he looked at Harry's and again looked at Preston. He opened the gate and allowed him in. Preston couldn't help but give a giant smile.

"I can't believe that worked," Harry said under his breath.

Preston once again grabbed him by the arm and took him inside.

Music was blaring from speakers, and the room vibrated a bit. It wasn't as crowded as he thought, which was a plus because he didn't want Harry having a full-blown panic attack on the dance floor.

He knew that this wouldn't be a drinking night for either of them. It was going to be a 'make Harry as calm as possible' night, which was most nights if he was being completely honest.

Preston tried to dance, but Harry was being sheepish.

"Will you just dance already?" Preston practically screamed.

No one seemed to notice, but Harry most definitely did.

"I'm... I... I'm... I'm... I'm trying... my... please don't... please don't yell... I'm sorry... I'm really sorry," Harry said.

He looked around and started to run in the direction of the bathroom.

Preston wanted to bang his head against the wall. He knew better than that with Harry. It wasn't fair that he got mad at him, yet, at the same time, Preston wondered if it was fair that he had to live his life on certain terms to ensure that Harry always felt comfortable. What was he saying? The Costa teen felt like a complete asshole.

SISTER MARY NEWMAN – JUNE 1968

Normally she exempted herself from visiting parishioners' homes on Sunday. She really preferred to just reflect on the day, which normally consisted of hundreds of members of Saint Agnes

Trying to use her as a form of confession. As a nun, she really didn't have the power to help give forgiveness. This town was just full of sin. She was sure that other towns were just as sinful, but there was just something about the citizens trying to slip her tips as if she could accept them. She would put them into the collection plates.

She was only in the Costa residence once several years back. Even then, it was an outdoor event in the backyard. This was her first time being inside the house. It was a nice house but definitely decorated for their Italian heritage. There was a smell of cigars and cigarettes that overpowered the home. What probably was a wonderful smelling lasagna cooking paled in comparison to the overall aroma.

Delia walked over. She looked pissed, which wasn't a

shocking look for her.

"Where are the Fitzpatrick's?" she spat out.

"This was supposed to be their dinner for whatever reason. Why are we here?" she said, clearly annoyed.

"I'm sure they will be here soon," Mary explained. "Where is Rodrick?" Not that Mary really wanted to see Rodrick, but still, she was shocked he wasn't forced to come himself.

"I grounded him. I'll explain later," Delia reluctantly explained.

Clearly, something was not being stated there.

The doorbell rang, and someone on the staff went to open the door. The staff consisted of relatives of the Costa family or people who potentially came off the boat with the Costa family. Regardless, Mary didn't trust any of them.

Susan walked over and smiled. "Hi!" she said.

She was too chipper. Mary didn't like that her friend was chipper. She was supposed to be sad. She was leaving them for San Francisco. This was going to be their last real get-together for the time being.

"Thank goodness you are here." Mary decided it was best to ditch the sorrow for the time being. She could yell at Susan later. "Is everything alright?" the Fitzpatrick daughter asked.

Mary shrugged, "Yes and no. It's just very uncomfortable. Luca has been talking with Benton since we arrived. I've just been sitting here in silence. Delia keeps looking at their wine collection, and I swear I saw her shed a tear."

Mary was always glad when Delia chose sobriety. However, the tear was just a bit too much.

"I'm going to miss this," Susan admitted.

Mary wanted to respond, then don't leave, but she wasn't going to be a jerk. For whatever reason, Susan felt the need to leave town, which was fine. She would miss her with all her heart but still.

"So, then you will be leaving tomorrow?" Mary asked.

Susan nodded. "Brandon will be driving me to the airport," she explained.

HARRY – JUNE 2019

Why would Preston yell at me? I know it is my fault. It's always my fault. That's why my mother isn't around because of me. Hope hates me because of my actions. Preston will hate me and break up with me, and Hannah or Aunt Vivica will have to come to pick me up. Then either one of them will end up in a fistfight with Jackie Carson-Costa on her front lawn. Or worse, Aunt Vivica's crazy maid, Holly, would get involved. I can't have this happen. No please don't break up with me, Preston. I need you in my life.

Harry was in tears in a bathroom stall. There was a good chance that two men were getting it on in a stall near him. He was trying his hardest not to pay attention to that.

This had to have been the filthiest bathroom he had ever been in. He went to West Grosse Pointe High School for a semester for one class, though, and that too had some really nasty bathrooms, but nothing compared to this. He heard someone else entering the bathroom, and he recognized the boy's shoes on the other side.

"Please let me in," Preston begged of him.

Harry wasn't sure that he wanted to let him in, though. "I'm not here," Harry proclaimed. He realized how dumb that sounded.

"I'm sorry," Preston told him.

The curly-haired boy was unsure if he would accept that apology, but he also wanted to accept it.

"I'm letting you in," he told Preston as he opened the stall.

Preston walked in, and looked around. "This is a filthy bathroom," he said and blinked a few times. "Look Harry, I'm sorry for being an asshole," his boyfriend told him.

Harry believed that he was sorry. It was just that he was legit hurt by his words.

"I just... there are... I'm sorry," Harry said as a singular tear ran down his cheek.

Preston wiped the tear for him. "Don't you dare ever tell me you are sorry for something like that again. You don't need to be sorry. I need to be sorry. I know you have insecurities. I just want you to loosen your shell a bit, so you aren't as insecure," Preston explained.

"I don't want to disappoint you. I'm really trying to get better, Preston. I really enjoy it when we do things that you like. Normally, it is a singular date where we try one new thing, and while I'm always nervous, it is easy. We are doing a new thing every few hours. You also normally know what the outcome will be. In this situation, you are learning it as you go," Harry told him.

Preston stretched himself, "I get it. I think that maybe this wasn't the ideal weekend for you. I should have thought this through a bit more.

Harry took a deep breath, "I want us to do new things together. I want us to be able to be a couple. I just don't see the need to be at a gay bar. The drag thing will be fun to watch, but this bar is not my scene. A straight bar wouldn't be my scene either. You know that."

Harry hoped that he realized that was the issue. It wasn't him being insecure about his sexuality. He was not comfortable around loud and large crowds, where drinking and probably drugs were all around them.

His boyfriend rubbed the back of his own neck and sighed. He looked Harry in the eyes. "I get it. Maybe this weekend should have been something I did on my own,"

Preston explained.

This sort of hurt Harry a little bit. "I want to try new experiences with you. It's just... did we really need to go to a gay bar in Chicago to experience new things? Weren't there any gay-friendly coffee houses or something that we could have tried? I would have been down for that," Harry said.

They both looked at one another with the same face.

"Ok... I at least would have tried to be down for it."

Preston laughed a bit and leaned in to kiss him on the lips. "I love you, Harry Knight," his boyfriend said.

Harry blushed and then kissed him back. "I love you, Preston Costa," he said back.

It was then that Harry realized that they were standing in a bathroom stall.

"Let's get out of here, please," Harry stated.

Preston nodded in agreement.

HARRY – JUNE 2019

The rest of the weekend went well. He actually enjoyed the drag pageant. It was definitely not something he saw himself doing in the future, but it was fun. He would go to another. Harry would even cheer Preston on if he ever tried to enter one.

There was only one incident, and that was when Harry briefly remembered an event from his childhood where his Aunt Vivica had entered both his cousin Laura and his sister Hope into a beauty pageant. The two girls went at it for weeks on end until neither won. Preston had to talk him down from that one.

It was honestly not a bad weekend after they both realized that they could co-exist and love one another without having to spend every moment together and enjoy things separately while respectfully supporting one another.

One of the things that Harry agreed on was that he needed to get better educated about queer people, if only for himself. His conversation with Lloyd and Christoff made him realize that he really had been living in a bubble. Harry liked living in that bubble, but it didn't mean he couldn't expand upon it.

The Knight boy looked at his phone and sighed. He and Langley would probably end up drifting apart. That was a sad reality. However, he got a text from Gena to hang out when he got back in town, and Harry said he was down. He just wished that Brad would potentially say something. A ping went off on his phone. It was a bit on the nose.... it was a text from Brad.

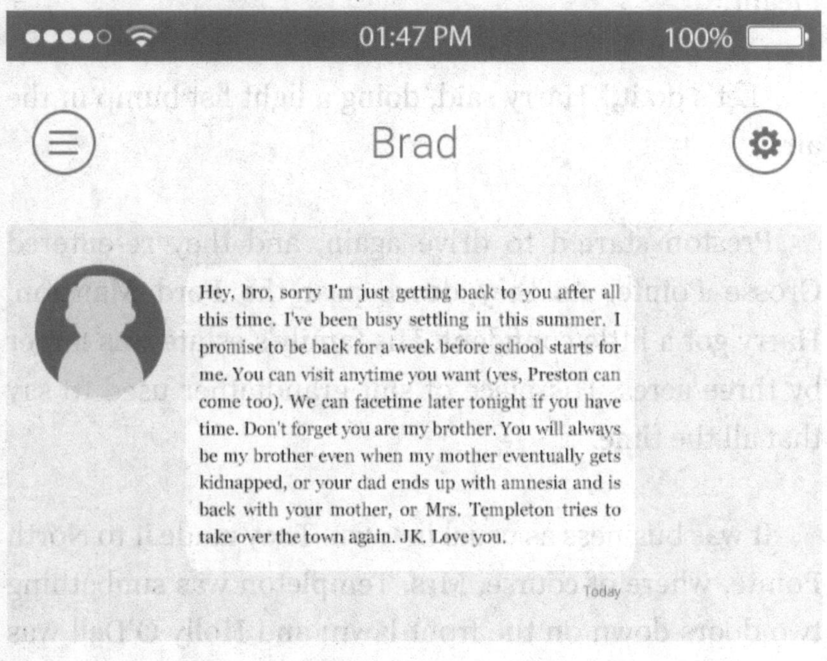

That message honestly made Harry take a deep breath and feel at ease for the first time in months. Preston was more than enough at this point for him. But knowing that Brad was out there thinking about him made him a little calmer.

They were still in the car when Preston stopped. They were at the city limit for Saint Clair Shores.

The Costa teen looked Harry in the eye. "You ready to re-enter the land of crazy?" he joked.

Harry chuckled a bit. Sadly, he knew exactly what he meant.

"Let's do it," Harry said, doing a light fist bump in the air.

Preston started to drive again, and they re-entered Grosse Pointe. As they drove past the Ford Mansion, Harry got a little confident. His family's estate was larger by three acres. His piece of shit grandfather used to say that all the time.

It was business as usual in town. They made it to North Pointe, where of course, Mrs. Templeton was sunbathing two doors down on the front lawn; and Holly O'Dell was screaming on the phone to get the situation under control.

Hannah walked out the front door and waved as she

saw the two boys pull in. Harry got out of the car and ran over to his older sister to hug her.

"Hey, how did things go?" Hannah asked cautiously.

Harry smiled at her. "It went great," he explained.

Hannah smiled at this. "I'm glad." She looked at her watch. "I actually have to get going. I have a meeting with Margot Fitzpatrick. I'll explain it to you later."

She blew him a kiss, and she ran to her car.

Preston ran over. "You want to hang out later?" he asked.

Harry nodded. "Yeah, you can come back over later, or we can go to your house if you want," Harry told him.

"You are always welcome at my house, but I never know what I'm walking into. Why don't we just make a date for here." Preston laughed as he said this.

"Sounds good."

The two boys kissed one another. His phone started to ping again and again and again and again...

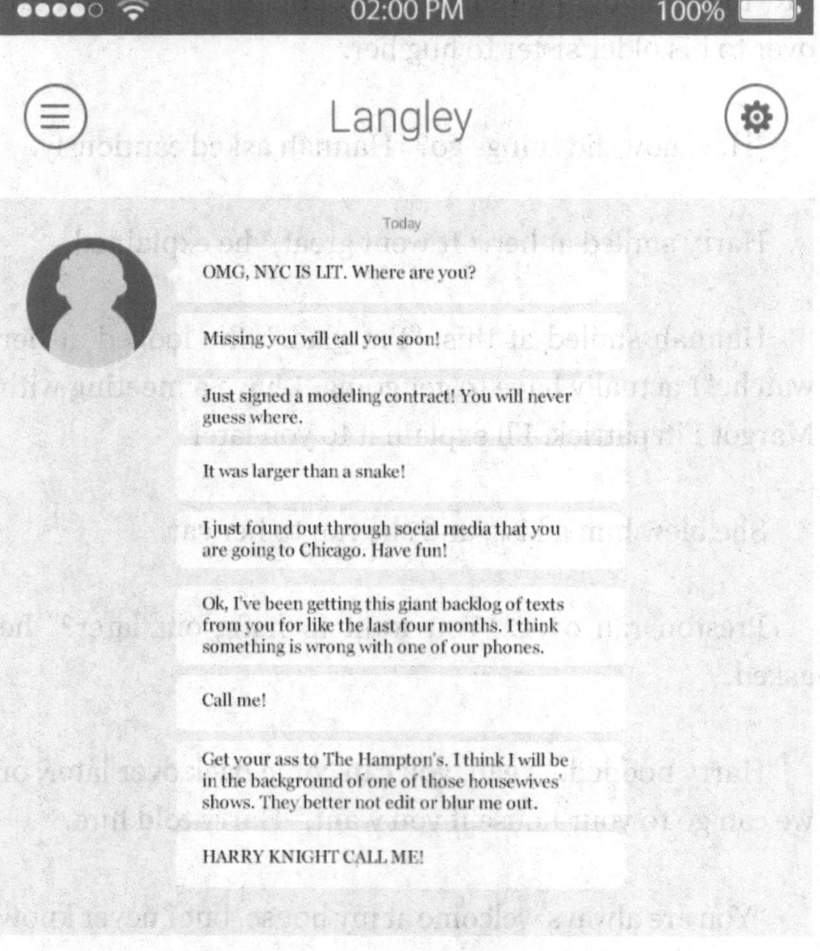

The messages kept on going. He quickly hit the call button on his phone.

"Langley? Oh my gosh, hey!"

SUSAN – JUNE 1968

It was not lost on Susan that Mary was acting a bit cold towards her. She somewhat understood. Yet, at the same time, she had no clue why it seemed to bother her on the level that it did. Mary had always been the calmest and most collected out of all of them. She was the voice of reason for the group.

"I can try calling you as soon as I get to the hotel I'll be staying at," she explained.

This did make Mary smile. "I would like that. I need to be your first call, after your parents, that is," the nun said.

Although she intended to call her mother, her father was still upset that she was leaving.

It was a bit annoying for Susan, to say the least. He was more upset over the fact that he would now need to hire someone to run the bar, which would mean probably paying them more. Nadia had already offered, but she was not eighteen yet. The bizarre part of it was that her father honestly had considered it.

Delia stormed over. She seemed sober still, so that was a positive.

"Ok, this evening is nothing like I thought it would be. Luca is definitely a really shady businessman, and I have many issues with this man, but this is just a really boring dinner party," the Knight matriarch explained.

Susan had to admit that it did seem to be the case.

"When are you leaving again?" Delia asked.

"Tomorrow," Susan said yet again. "It's the end of an era."

"Are you bitches done chatting it up in the middle of the foyer?" a familiar voice asked as they all turned around.

Mrs. Templeton was standing there with a drink. "I was told that you should all join us in the dining room." She then walked off.

Susan looked at both Delia and Mary. "Where did she come from?" she asked.

"Some say she was hatched," Mary explained.

Susan and Delia both looked at Mary.

"Oh, you mean right now? I have no idea. I hadn't seen her earlier in the evening," the nun shrugged.

The three women all went into the dining room. It was a rather impressive affair. Susan assumed that it was decorated with Italian artifacts or things from when they lived in Italy, regardless of price point. There were definitely things in there that her mother probably would have bought at a rummage sale because she thought they were expensive, which was why her father had banned her from rummage sales. Also, he felt it made them look poor.

Susan sat down next to Brandon and Nadia on the one side, and Mary sat next to her on her other side. The plates were all gold in color. It didn't mean they were real gold in actuality.

She looked over to Delia and Benton. They both seemed to find the room a bit overkill, which made sense. Everything from North Pointe was the best of the best. If anything, it was almost as if the

Costa mansion was trying to emulate Northland even though the home's structure was completely different.

"So, I hear that little Susan will be leaving for out West tomorrow," Luca stated at the head of the table as he took a sip of his wine.

Seamus coughed, "Well, she is. But I don't like it." His Irish dialect became very strong.

"Oh, the girl is far from little, and you should be happy for her," Delia stated. Even her Hispanic dialect, which she tried very hard to hide, was coming out.

Seamus shot her a dirty look.

Benton looked in Seamus' direction, and he quickly turned back around. A Knight was always the one person that could get Seamus to retract his claws when someone went against his views on things. Knights could do no wrong. Susan hoped that they did not feel the same about the Costa family.

"Well, regardless. I have family out there. You should call upon them if you ever need anything," Luca explained.

Susan probably would have taken him up on his offer if he was any other person. He wasn't, though, and that was the deal-breaker.

The evening honestly dragged on. The Costa family were hardly people who should be trusted. However, for Susan, she wasn't as worried about leaving her family around them. The Strawberry blonde could tell the same was not to be said from Delia about the Knight family, which was understandable. The Knights had their own money. The Fitzpatrick's were still trying to figure out how to keep the money piling in.

PRESTON – JUNE 2019

As he walked into the foyer of his house, he smelled the familiar aroma of lasagna. His father had been cooking. He peaked into his dad's office, but he wasn't there; however, his uncle Jack was.

"Hey." Preston said.

"Hey yourself," Uncle Jack said back. He gestured for him to come on in.

"So, did it go over well?" Jack asked.

Preston shrugged as he put his luggage down. "It went like I thought it would. I mean, we definitely feel closer to one another, and I'm happy," Preston smiled.

Uncle Jack was not much for smiling, but he gave a slight grimace.

"Good. See things work out in the long run," Jack told him.

Preston was about to respond when his mother ran into the room.

"Oh my gosh, you are home!" she said as she hugged him from behind.

Preston was happy to hear his mother's voice and had to admit that it was nice not to listen to it for a few days as well.

The Costa teen turned around. "It's nice to see you," he said a bit awkwardly.

"Oh, so you aren't going to tell me how your weekend went, but you will tell your Uncle Jack? I see how it is. I'll let you talk, and then I'll force it out of Jack later," Jackie said as she walked out of the room.

"I never tell her anything," Jack explained.

Preston smiled, "I know you don't."

His uncle was waiting for his explanation of the events.

"It was a mess, but I knew it would be. Harry's not someone who likes to leave his comfort zone." Preston explained.

Jack shuffled a bit on the bed. "Well, will that be a problem for the two of you?" he asked.

Preston thought about it for a moment. Would it be?

"I don't think. I have to be honest; the more I opened up to him, he opened up back to me. We had real conversations that went into depth. Maybe there is more out there than just Grosse Pointe. But Harry Knight is in Grosse Pointe."

"You aren't going to settle because of his insecurities. That's not the Preston that I know," Jack reminded him.

Preston shot him a look. "Absolutely not. I might love Harry, but that doesn't mean I'd ever let him hold me back," Preston explained.

"Thank goodness!" Jackie said as she poked her head in.

Preston rolled his eyes. It didn't shock him at all that she was listening in.

"Really, mom?" he asked her.

Jackie sighed. "I just want you to be cautious. I've told you the stories about the Knight family. The best thing the Fitzpatrick's ever did was to kick Vivica out of their family," she expressed.

Preston once again rolled his eyes. "You know very well that isn't what happened. Harry's aunt is still a member of that family. Besides, Nial Fitzpatrick is a tool along with his sister Margot. I can't believe for a second that they are the children of Nadia and Brandon," Preston admitted.

HARRY – JUNE 2019

"So, you will be seeing Langley at the end of next month and Brad next week then?" Hannah asked as they sat in the drawing-room at North Pointe after Harry was done with unpacking.

"Yeah. I'm excited to see both of them. I'm not sure how it will be dodging the subject of one another, but still," Harry explained.

"Oh, please... those two are far from over. They broke up how many times over the course of a year and a half? Let them grow up a little bit," Hannah explained.

It was nice to be back home. Harry had to admit that the drag stuff wasn't terrible. He was still getting used to this new queer world. There was still a large part of him that didn't know if he wanted to embrace it. At least not on the level that Preston did. However, he would support Preston one hundred and ten percent with whatever he chose to do.

He never really thought of the possibility that Preston

might one day dress in clothing that was traditionally for females. However, if that day came, Harry was ready to hold his hand tight as they walked down the street together.

"Have you heard from aunt Vivica or dad?" Harry asked.

Hannah nodded. "I mean, I text them mostly because of KMC related things. However, Holly has been giving me the play-by-play of their whole European adventure. I'm honestly shocked she hasn't been blocked by them yet," Hannah rolled her eyes.

Harry couldn't help but laugh, "Oh, please. If aunt Vivica ignored her messages for more than an hour, Holly would be on the next trip to Europe, calling every embassy to start a search party."

They both laughed at this.

"So, what are your plans for tomorrow?" Hannah inquired.

Harry shrugged. "I think I will visit Sister Mary Newman for a little bit. I haven't seen her since the end of the school year."

He had a few questions for the nun. She had given him a diary of her late friend Susan Fitzpatrick, and he had recently finished reading it. It stopped so abruptly, but the dates didn't match up to when she died. He was craving more of her story.

Hannah's phone started to ring. She looked down at it. "I need to take this," she told her brother.

Harry smiled and got up. He walked out of the drawing-room and into the North Pointe Foyer and looked around the room. There was so much history attached to this house. So, many crazy things had happened in this room alone. His great-grandfather was shot at the top of the staircase sometime in the early '70s. His aunt and mother had gotten into fistfights in this room. His father and sometimes uncle had also gotten into fistfights themselves. This was his life. It was a pretty iconic life.

Would he one day inherit North Pointe along with his sisters? Probably. Would he want to live here into his fifties as his father had? Probably not. Harry had no idea what the future held with Preston, but he did know that he wanted to spend it with him or for as long as he possibly could with him.

SUSAN – JUNE 1968

The next morning Susan awoke early. She was all packed and arranged for her things to arrive in San Francisco within the next day.

This would be the last time she would walk into the current living room. Depending on how long she was gone, their new home might be finished by the time she returned.

The Fitzpatrick daughter looked at her parents. She immediately hugged her mother. She and Ida had never really had much in common, but she still loved her mother completely.

"I love you," her mother said.

"I love you too," Susan told her, and she meant it.

She looked at her father. "I don't want you to be mad at me," she told him.

Seamus took a deep breath, "I'm not mad at you. I could never be mad at you. I'm just not ready to lose my little girl."

Again, with the little girl line, Susan gave her father a hug.

"We will see each other again," the daughter promised her father.

There was a chill in the room when she said this.

She heard a honk. It must have been Brandon being impatient.

She looked at her parents one last time. "I will call you once I land," Susan explained.

She grabbed her purse and put her coat on. It was time.

As she walked out, Brandon's car was nowhere to be found. Instead, a Knight limo was in the driveway. The window rolled down, and Susan looked inside. Delia, Mary, Brandon, and Nadia were all sitting inside.

"What, did you think we weren't going to see you off to the airport?" Delia asked.

Susan opened the door to the limo and got inside. She sat down next to Mary. The two women looked at one another and smiled.

"We are ready," Delia told the driver.

This was it. They drove out of the driveway and started to go. They passed Nadia's house... David Brash was taking his son DJ on a walk outside. They drove past Saint Agnes; Mrs. Templeton was yelling at a squirrel while holding an ice cream cone.

As they furthered out, they drove past the Fitzpatrick Bar. Susan couldn't help but shed a tear.

Mary took her hand, and Delia took the other. Mary would never be her girlfriend, wife, lover, or anything romantic, but she would remain one of the loves of her life. So would Delia, even if she never felt romantic about her. These two women were her soulmates.

HARRY – JUNE 2019

The next day Harry woke up to the smell of breakfast made by his sister Hannah. She had left by the time he woke up, but she made sure to make him something. The house's head maid Holly O'Dell had already eaten half the meal herself. Harry liked Holly, but he wanted to know what her family thought she was doing at this job all day. Did she go home and claim that she was overworked? Probably if he was being honest.

He decided to walk to the library at Saint Agnes, mostly because it was such a nice day. Preston would pick him up later. The Knight boy walked into the library and could see the nun wheeling a cart of books towards the shelves.

He briskly walked over. "Sister Mary Newman!" he said with a smile.

The nun turned to him. "Harry. How is my favorite bookworm doing?" she asked with an equally large smile.

"Good. I'm sorry I haven't been around much since the school year ended."

This made her laugh. "Harry, summer is for relaxing and having fun. I can't expect to see you here every day."

She gestured for him to sit down, which he did. She sat next to him.

"I know. I guess I used to," Mary nodded.

"Yes. Yes, you did. If I remember correctly, you and that Kinglsey girl spent most of your summer at the pool last year."

Harry had to admit that he had forgotten about that.

"I just heard from Langley yesterday," he explained.

Mary nodded.

"Oh right, I forgot you don't like Langley," Harry pointed out.

This made the nun laugh. "There are few people in this world I dislike. Langley is not one of them. I just have memories of that girl being a new-aged version of your aunt in my classroom last year," the nun admitted.

"I actually wanted to ask you something. Do you remember the diaries you gave me a few years back? I recently finished them. I was wondering if there was more to them, though," Harry explained.

This made Mary smile with fondness. "Oh, Susan. There isn't a day that goes by that I don't think of Susan or your great-grandmother. Two strong and courageous women," she explained.

"Susan's story is so wild to read. I can't believe that she managed to run the Fitzpatrick Bar essentially by herself after her parents went and started the steel company full-time; Or is it technically because of her that the full-blown feud between my family and the Fitzpatrick's started?" Harry rambled on.

Mary laughed. "Yes, Susan definitely could be the hero when she wanted," Mary stated.

The nun looked up at the window for a moment. "I don't have any more of Susan's diaries. However, I have some old letters that she sent when she moved away for a few years."

This left Harry a bit sad. He had really enjoyed getting to know her inner thoughts. However, he looked forward to the concept of reading further into her life regardless.

"I have another question for you," Harry admitted out

loud.

Sister Mary Newman smiled. "What is it, my child?" she asked with genuine intrigue.

"Do you think that my great-grandmother would have been happy with how I've turned out or the way my family has turned out in general? She died when I was a lot younger. Susan spoke of her often and her disdain for how my great-grandfather and grandfather had been."

He really wondered if Delia Knight would have been ok with who he was as a person.

Mary stayed quiet for a moment. "Your grandmother was a complicated person with her own demons. She married into a family that didn't accept her and then didn't accept her own son's future wife. By the time your father had been born, she truly was a reformed person. She loved your father and the man that he became. She questioned many of his choices along the way, but they were always his choices," Mary admitted to him. "If you are referring to the fact that you are gay, your grandmother constantly tried to find women for Susan after she came back to town. I really don't think she would have cared. She would have been concerned over you dating a Costa, but I think she would see that you two care for one another."

Harry looked over at the door, and Preston was standing there.

Mary turned and looked herself. "I have some work to get done," Mary said as she rose from her seat.

Harry did as well.

"Oh, Sister Mary Newman. I know my family would love to have you over for dinner soon," Harry explained.

Mary turned back to look at him, "Dinner with the Knight family? I'd love to." She smiled and returned to her work.

Preston walked over and waved at Harry. "Hey. How was your first night back?" he asked his boyfriend.

Harry smiled. "It was pretty good. Hannah and I spent some time together, and Langley called me five times with gossip from New York," he explained.

The Knight boy could tell that Preston was in a good mood.

"What do you have planned for us for the rest of the day?" he asked.

Preston had a devilish look on his face. "I may or may not have gotten us tickets to a drag show in Detroit," he admitted.

Harry nodded. "Alright, but tomorrow. We are going to the yacht club. I called Gena. They are going to have lunch with us, that is if you don't mind," he explained.

Preston looked a little bashful for once.

"That actually sounds amazing, Mr. Knight."

He held out his hand, and Harry took it. Harry waved to Sister Mary Newman as they left. Summer was far from over for the two teens, and they were about to make every moment count.

JULY 15, 1968

*D*ear Mary, It's been several weeks since I've been in San Francisco. It's such a different environment. In many ways, it's more open, but in many ways, it isn't.

I miss you. I miss my family. I miss Delia. People don't believe me about Mrs. Templeton.

It didn't take me long to get a job as a bartender. It's an establishment that I can only describe as being male-oriented, but the clientele is not interested in me in the slightest.

I think you would like it out here. You always said that Grosse Pointe and you never fit together. It might be something to think about.

I hope that things are going well. I know that we talk on the phone practically every other day, but I trust that you are watching after Delia. I know that you are keeping an eye on my parents as well.

Make sure to give Brandon a stern talking to about his love life every once in a while. That Nadia girl is incredible but also so free-spirited in a way that I can only dream of being.

Potentially one day, I will move back. Maybe by then, the world will be a more open place. Grosse Pointe might be a more open place. Dare I say it, maybe the Knight and Fitzpatrick families will get along one day.

I love you always,

Susan F.

ACKNOWLEDGEMENTS

I would like to thank first and foremost my former artist luviiilove. This will be our final physical book collaboration and the front cover art is phenomenal! I wish you luck on all your future endeavors. VWebs123 the team responsible for the promo video also was able to clone an old promotional picture for "The Innocent Years" and create a new likeminded back cover image for this book as well. My format person, Polyarts36 also deserves a special shoutout for bringing my vision for the cover further into reality. Finally, my editor and proofreader; Sandra Watts who did her job all while having a broken arm and then getting surgery and had to patiently wait as I reconfigured where I wanted to take the plot of this book over the course of a year practically.

I'd like to give shout outs to the following people as well for being in my support system in one way or another as I've written this book. Nikki Baker, Josh Patterson, Sue Ann Facey, Ryan Welsh, and Britney.

As always, my biggest appreciation goes to the readers. Whether this is your first novel or your sixth novel you have read of mine thank you so much!

ABOUT THE AUTHOR

L A Michaels (He/ Him) is a Michigan-born and raised author who also lived in Kansas and South Carolina while in high school. L A worked for the TVMegaSite for over ten years, writing recaps and summaries for daytime TV. L A is also the author of the "Between Heaven and Hell" series as well as the novel "I Love You, I Hate You, I Miss You." When L A is not writing, he watches theatre, drag, old movies, and reading comics or reading other books himself.

Twitter: lamichaels1995

Instagram: lamichaelsauthor

Facebook: L A Michaels

Goodreads: L A Michaels

Follow my artist Luviiilove on their DeviantArt account of the same name! Checkout my new artist Milkaela on Instagram @_milkaela.